Waiting a Lifetime Copy

MICHELE E. GWYNN

AN M.E. GWYNN PUBLICATION

Copyright © 2015, Second Edition (2024) by Michele E. Gwynn

All rights reserved.

This story is a work of fiction. All characters, settings, and situations are products of the author's imagination and in no way are representative of or related to real persons. No portion of this book may be reproduced in any form without written permission from the publisher or author, except as permitted by U.S. copyright law.

Introduction

Welcome, readers.

Waiting a Lifetime began as a short story written for a multi-author, limited time anthology. As such, it was limited then by word count for inclusion in the collaboration, and when the anthology was eventually unpublished, I published the short story myself. However, I always felt it was unfinished. The time finally arrived, and my muse nagged me to make it the story it was always meant to be, a mystical romance with all the emotional drama the characters deserved, and the ending it should always have had. I hope you enjoy Wade and Melissa's story, one that spans the very fabric of time...

~Michele

Contents

Epigraph		1
1.	Chapter 1	3
2.	Chapter 2	15
3.	Chapter 3	31
4.	Chapter 4	45
5.	Chapter 5	55
6.	Chapter 6	67
7.	Chapter 7	83
8.	Chapter 8	91
9.	Chapter 9	97
10.	Chapter 10	109
11.	Chapter 11	119
12.	Chapter 12	123
13.	Chapter 13	131

14.	Chapter 14	139
15.	Chapter 15	147
16.	Chapter 16	155
17.	Chapter 17	165
18.	Chapter 18	179
19.	Chapter 19	189
20.	Chapter 20	197
Book Freebie!		205
Also By Michele E. Gwynn		209

Sophocles famously stated that fate has a terrible power, that neither wealth nor war will help one escape it, no walls can keep it out, and nothing can outrun it, but whether that's a good thing remains to be seen...

Chapter 1

Pelican's Bay, Florida, Summer, 2005

"You forgot this," a voice not unfamiliar to Melissa called out as she maneuvered her crutches to turn back around.

The smile that greeted her made her blush. It wasn't a feeling she was comfortable with, so she lowered her head allowing her long brown hair to swing forward and hide her face.

"Thanks." Melissa muttered the word, almost too low for human hearing. She reached out and took the plastic bag filled with apples that she left behind in the grocery store from the young man's hand. Readjusting it on her wrist, she once again leaned onto the metal hand-crutch and turned to leave.

"Wait. You're Jed's little sister, right?"

"Melissa."

He grinned. "That's right. I've seen you a couple of times when I've come by." He extended his hand. "I'm Wade."

Melissa looked at his big, rugged hand sticking out there waiting to be shaken, then glanced up at his face. Wade Walker. Of course, she knew his name. His green eyes contained more of a smile than his lips, which was to say, a lot. He stood more than a foot taller than her own height of five foot four inches. His dirty-blond hair held a slight curl and was a little longer than it probably should be. He needed a haircut, but he was so handsome that Melissa barely noticed anything else. Again, she repositioned her weight, and after leaning her crutch against her side, offered her hand. His large one immediately swallowed up her small one. His grip was strong, and his skin was warm to the touch.

"Nice to meet you." Her soft voice didn't carry far. Melissa quickly let go, embarrassed. She grabbed her crutch, preparing to leave.

"Likewise. Seems like we should've met before now. Need some help out?"

Before Melissa could say no, Wade scooped up the three bags she had hanging on her left arm and slipped them off her wrist while simultaneously holding her crutch, so it wouldn't fall. He handed it back immediately and began walking alongside the quiet girl.

"Where's that brother of yours today?"

"He's in class." Melissa ambulated to her car feeling more self-conscious than she had in years. Each step reminded her that she didn't have full use of her legs. She'd grown up this way after the car accident that robbed her of her ability to walk ten years earlier. She still couldn't remember the details of the wreck, only sitting in the backseat, coloring pictures, while her mom and dad argued about his drinking. All memories beyond that were nonexistent until she'd awakened in a stark white room in the hospital. Doctors said the paralysis was permanent, but her mom never gave up on her. Therapists worked with her daily, and almost a year later, Melissa was able to take a few steps using a walker. The next year, most of the feeling returned to her legs. At first, it hurt like hell, like all the nerves in her legs woke up at the same time and experienced the crash all over again, but with continued exercise, the pain began to recede. Three years after the accident, she'd graduated to hand crutches and had used them since. Her left leg was more stable than the right, but in all, she was lucky. She could've been in a wheelchair for life. Usually, she didn't notice her disability, but ever since Jed began bringing his new buddy Wade around, she'd been aware of every single inch of the two metal poles that went with her everywhere. At this moment, she wished with all her heart that she could walk normally beside this handsome young man.

"Oh, yeah, it's Tuesday. Isn't that his engineering class?" Wade reached her truck first, and taking the keys from her hand, opened it so he could reach across and put the bags on the passenger seat. Then, he stepped back and waited as Melissa got in.

"Yeah. It's his favorite class this semester." She pulled the crutches inside and put them on the passenger-side floorboard where they leaned onto the seat.

"He loves tinkering with stuff," Wade said as he pulled the seatbelt down and reached across Melissa's body, clicking it into place.

She froze. "Uh huh."

Wade glanced up, green eyes twinkling. "There. Now you're safe." He straightened and made sure she was tucked in, nothing hanging out.

"Well, it was nice to finally meet you. Come out and say hi sometime when I come by."

Melissa half-smiled, unable to hold eye contact any longer. She feared she'd suffocate from lack of oxygen. "Sure."

"Cool. Take care now." Wade closed her door and jogged back inside Pelican's Market.

Melissa knew he worked there, but this was the first time she'd come face to face with him. It was the first time he'd spoken to her. Whenever he came around the house with Jed, she disappeared into her room, always avoiding him. It was just too hard. He was really handsome. Her mom loved him. Jed said he was the best person he knew, and Melissa could see why her family liked him. She liked him too…from a distance. But the way she felt when he was within the same breathing space made her remember every single thing about herself that was wrong.

Wade was popular in their community, and she knew he was dating Arlene Richards. The couple had been going out together since high school. He'd probably marry her and have beautiful babies. That wasn't something Melissa could offer. The injury to her pelvis had done far more damage than just her legs. She was sixteen when she found out she would never be able to conceive naturally. Then, it hadn't seemed to matter, but as she grew older, that fact fixed firmly in her mind whenever she bothered to entertain a stray thought about a boy. Now that she was nineteen, she figured she was the oldest virgin she knew and likely to stay that way. Who wanted damaged goods?

Her own father hadn't wanted her.

After the accident, he couldn't seem to handle all the surgeries Melissa had to go through. He couldn't even look at her. He drank more, and finally, having had enough, her mother, Katherine Ryan, kicked her father, Bob, out. She hadn't seen him since. It was just Melissa, her mom, and Jed.

Jed was her hero. He protected Melissa, encouraged her to try new things, and not let two metal poles stop her from doing whatever the heck she wanted to do. He always told her, *"There ain't a thing wrong with you, Mel, except inside your own head."* Jed was two years older and working his way through college. He had decided he wanted to be an engineer, but specifically, a medical engineer for prosthetics and gadgets to help people like his little sister. He was always coming up with ideas and had even built a homemade hydraulic lift to the room above the garage that he'd converted into his own private bachelor pad. Melissa usually took the stairs, not because she didn't trust her brother's invention to get her safely from the ground to the second-floor landing, but because she was stubborn and wanted to do things as normally as possible. So. Jed used it. His friends used it, too, especially after a night of beer and poker. They all thought it was great fun.

Melissa cranked the engine and put the truck in gear. She slowly let off the hand brake and reversed out of the parking space. Once she cleared the car next to her, she put the Chevy in DRIVE and squeezed the handle for the gas pedal. Her truck was tricked out with hand controls. She'd only recently passed her driver's test and was feeling the joy of freedom and independence, not having to wait for her mother to drive her somewhere or for Jed to give her a lift. Specialized driver's education taught her how to operate a vehicle with hand controls, and the state of Florida installed what she needed on her own brand-spanking-new-to-her used truck. The old Chevy cost nearly all the money she'd saved from her photography sales, but it was worth it. Now she could get around and take even more pictures to sell to various magazines and sites online seeking visuals for their websites and articles. She'd already earned back nearly a third of what she'd spent on the old truck. That feeling of security meant the world to her. It proved she could take care of herself.

As she pulled onto the road, her mind went back over the entire conversation with Wade. She hadn't added much worthwhile to it, but each word he spoke got locked away inside her mental treasure chest. The fact that he made a point to introduce himself to her after she'd shied away from meeting him at her own home surprised her. Guys like Wade didn't make time for girls like her. Guys like Wade had perfect girlfriends like Arlene Richards, with her blonde hair and perfect legs. But he'd spared a moment for her, and although it caused her to be painfully self-conscious, some of it was kind of nice. When he leaned over her to connect the seatbelt, she could smell his cologne. It was light and pleasant, whatever it was, but that, combined with the scent of the shampoo in his hair, was fantastic. Melissa wished she could have just taken a deep breath right then and there, but instead, she'd frozen in place like a deer caught in headlights. She'd been afraid to move let alone breathe. It was such an odd thing for him to do, but she would never forget it. She knew he was just being nice to his friend's little sister, but it was still the closest she'd ever been to a boy, and she knew she'd never forget a single minute of it.

The store had been busy all day, and Wade was ready to go home. As the assistant manager, he floated around quite a bit checking up on the cashiers and baggers, filling in whenever necessary, and handling customers with concerns and complaints. The store manager, Trey Hiccock, sat behind his desk on his over-sized butt most of his shift supervising Wade in between surfing the web for porn. Trey was middle-aged, married to his high school sweetheart—the only girl he'd ever dated—and probably the biggest dork Wade had ever known. He wasn't terribly bright, but he'd been working at Pelican's Market since he was sixteen. The man began as a summer bag boy and worked his way up the ladder through sheer complacency having never once searched for another job. Because of this, and because Wade figured Trey surely didn't have the most exciting life a man could have, he cut him some slack for indulging in voyeurism and goofing off instead of working. The guy had put in his time and made it to the highest position within the store, and he'd probably hold onto this job until he dropped dead. Wade had no intention of following in his footsteps.

His plans included leaving south Florida in August to begin his first year at Boston University School of Law. He'd just completed his Bachelor of Business degree and was working throughout the summer to save money for travel expenses. Thankfully, his dad was providing his first year's tuition, but after that, it was going to be up to Wade to provide the rest. He was going to be very busy over the next two to three years working his butt off while learning law. It wasn't going to be easy, but he was determined to complete his Juris Doctorate and enter the world of finance law. His girlfriend, Arlene, understood although she constantly nagged him about their relationship, how it wouldn't survive their being apart, and the long wait before they could get married. Wade smiled to himself as he thought about the way she would pout and run her fingers over his chest as she tried to sway him from his plan.

"But Wade..." She would always begin with those two words. *"If we're apart, you're going to forget all about me. Who's going to hold me and kiss me, and other things?"* At this point, she would already be pressed up against him, her ample bosom lightly rubbing back and forth across his own chest driving him a little crazy. The moment she saw desire flare in his green eyes, she'd pounce. *"I know! I could come with you, and we could live together!"*

For some reason, that was always a bucket of cold water, and he would back up and hold her hands between them creating a little breathing space.

"Baby, we've already talked about this. I'll either be in class or at work the entire time. I won't have any time in between for us. It's only two, maybe three years max. We can do it. It's going to set us up for our future together. Don't you love me, Arlene? Don't you want a big wedding, with all the trimmings? A house? Babies?" Then he'd lean in and plant a hot kiss on her soft lips. It worked every time.

"Of course I do, but—"

"No buts. Just tell me you love me, and then come here," he'd whisper, and they'd fall into each other's arms.

Those were Wade's plans, and he was determined everything should fall into place. He kept his routine tight with only a little time now and again to cut loose for some fun. That's where Jed Ryan came in. Jed was a great friend, and whenever Wade got too wrapped up in adult pursuits, Jed would appear and whisk him off for some very immature recreation. He was a good guy, Jed, and despite his love for cutting up, he had a good head on his shoulders and a kind heart. That was probably due in part to his sister Melissa. She was a shy one. Wade couldn't quite figure her out. Jed talked about his sister a lot. He always had good things to say. He praised how smart she was, how artistic, independent, and funny his little sister happened to be, but whenever Wade had come around, she was a ghost, nowhere to be found. And the few times he'd seen her, she'd quickly gone inside her room and stayed there until he left. Seemed she didn't like him very much and he couldn't understand why.

So, when he saw her today at work, he decided to formally introduce himself. When he noticed she'd left one of her bags on the counter, he jumped on the opportunity and rushed over to help. He was surprised when he finally saw her up close. Melissa Ryan was a very pretty girl. Long, shiny brown hair hung down in thick waves framing a sweet face. Her skin was so perfect, and looked so soft, he fought the urge to reach out and touch her cheek. But it was her eyes that struck him profoundly. Large brown eyes surrounded by long black lashes peeked shyly up at him from behind the cascade of her hair. He'd seen a lot in her eyes, in that moment. Uncertainty, intelligence, and just a hint of interest. Well, if he was honest with himself, it was the blush on her cheeks that told him that much. It was kind of cute, and it was then he decided to walk her out to her truck just to have a little bit more time with her. He had no idea what came over him when he made the move to buckle her into her seat. That was a bold breach of personal space, but the barest hint of her perfume, and the awareness that sprang up between them prodded the little devil inside to turn and smile not more than three inches from her very surprised face. It was worth it.

Wade got the feeling that Melissa hadn't had much interaction with the opposite sex, if the way she acted around him was any indication. Which was too bad, in his estimation, because she seemed like a nice girl. Even on crutches, she had a nice figure. He'd noticed. Hell, he was a guy, after all. But their brief encounter was probably the first time he'd forgotten about all his plans. All he could think about were the ways in which he could put a smile on Melissa Ryan's lovely lips.

The minutes ticked by while he was lost in thought.

"Hey, you plannin' on working all night or are you going to clock out?" Trey startled him out of his reverie. Apparently, time had marched on, and it was now ten minutes past the end of his shift.

"I must be more tired than I thought." Wade laughed it off and headed to the office to punch out.

As he walked to his car his phone buzzed in his pocket. He pulled it out and glanced at the screen. It was Jed.

"What's up, man?" he answered.

"Hey, you up for dinner at my place tonight? I've got some steaks, and they are meeting their maker on the barbecue pit in about forty-five minutes."

Wade's stomach rumbled at the word steaks. He chuckled. "Yeah, I suppose I could be persuaded to eat, but it's going to be an early night, man. I'm dog-tired and have to work in the morning."

"That's cool. I have a meeting with my advisor tomorrow, so no hijinks tonight. Just food. Bring Arlene. Plenty to eat here."

Wade hesitated. "Naw, man. Just me. I'd have to go and pick her up, and it takes her forever to get ready, not to mention she'd want to either stay late or go out afterwards."

Jed snorted. "Women. I get it."

"Hey, I saw your sister today." Wade slid into the driver's seat and cranked the engine of his Toyota Truck.

"You saw Mel? Well, she's been getting out a lot now that she has her license and a truck. Good for her."

"Yeah, she actually spoke to me."

"No kidding?" Jed was surprised. He knew his sister was shy around Wade for some reason. To date, she hadn't even said hello to his friend even though Jed had him around often enough.

"To be fair, I kind of chased her down. She'd forgotten one of her bags."

"I see. Well, maybe now that you've broken the ice, she might come out and eat with us. She's making the salad now."

Hearing that Melissa might join them brought a smile to Wade's face. He didn't know why, but suddenly, dinner at the Ryans held even more appeal than just a tasty grilled steak.

"Well, I guess I should be there in about twenty minutes then. You need anything? Beer? Salad dressing?"

"Nope. Got everything. Just bring your appetite."

"All right. See ya in a few." Wade hung up and pulled out of the parking lot. He turned up the radio and began to sing along to Aerosmith's *'Walk This Way'*. He had a feeling he hadn't experienced in a while. Anticipation. With all his planning and focus on work and college, he'd forgotten what it felt like to not exactly know what might happen next. Even though it was nothing big, just his curiosity to see if he could make Melissa Ryan blush again, he felt alive. Until this moment, he hadn't realized he'd been on autopilot.

Chapter 2

Melissa cut the tomatoes making sure to scoop out the goopy seeds. After dicing two ripe, red Beefeaters, she grabbed a cucumber and began peeling it. The cucumber met the sharp side of her knife and was sliced into perfect rounds. Shredded carrots followed, but no onions. She didn't like onions much. At least, not raw.

"Did you get the guts out of the 'maters?" Jed came up behind her and looked over her shoulder.

"Of course I did. I know you don't like the seeds."

"They're disgusting. Like tomato poop."

Melissa laughed. "Great. Now I'll be visualizing a tomato pooping on my salad."

"Make sure to have some extra."

"Why?"

"In case anyone comes by." Jed withheld the fact that Wade was on his way. He hated it when Melissa retreated to her room. He didn't see any reason for it, so he figured if she was caught out, she might stay out. It would be good for her to socialize a little bit. Other than himself and their mom, she didn't talk to many people. He didn't think that was at all healthy. And Wade was a good guy. Since they'd actually spoken earlier, she might feel a little more at ease around him now.

"Like who?" Melissa broke up the iceberg lettuce while looking over her shoulder at her brother. He was acting cagey.

"I don't know. Just sayin'." He reached into the fridge. "You want a beer?" He pulled out a bottle of Bud.

"You know I don't like beer. Tastes gross."

"It'll put hair on your chest." He winked.

"Ugh, Jed! I do not need hair on my chest, thank you."

Laughing, Jed poked her in the side. "Yeah, guys don't like hairy-chested chicks."

Melissa threw her elbow backwards and hit her brother in the gut.

"What was that for?" He looked surprised, and then calculating.

Uh oh.

"You deserved it. Talking about hairy-chested women…" Melissa tried to back up, but it was too late.

"Tickle attack!" Jed shouted the warning too late. He dug his fingers into her sides, relentlessly tormenting her in that way big brothers do.

"Stop! Jed!" Melissa screeched as she grabbed the counter to keep from falling over, although Jed would never let her fall.

"Stop what? I'm not doing anything...except tickling you!" The attack continued.

"Mom! Stop it, Jed. I'm going to pee!"

"What is going on in here?" Kate Ryan walked into her kitchen and found what she usually found, her son tormenting his sister. It wasn't a bad thing. Jed and Melissa got along better than any mother could ask for, but sometimes, she still had to break them up. Jed never knew when to quit, and there was at least one time when they were children that Melissa had, indeed, peed her pants during one of Jed's famous 'tickle attacks'.

"Jedidiah Michael Ryan, let your sister be! I don't want to be cleaning urine up off my kitchen floor."

Kate Ryan stood with a hand on her somewhat plump hip. She was a woman of medium height, medium weight, and a glare that could make the worst kind of sinner confess like he was on death row. Her mid-length brown hair was streaked with silver, and her brown eyes twinkled showing she wasn't mad although her tone was sharp. Jed hesitated, his hands poised to resume tickling his sister.

"That's enough, Jed, unless you want a pee salad."

"Aw, mom!" Jed immediately dropped his hands.

"Don't *'Aw, mom'* me. Go out there and flip those steaks before you burn them. I want mine medium-well, not charbroiled. Go on." She shooed him away.

"Salad's ready." Melissa resumed tossing the vegetables with the wooden salad forks.

"Is Jed putting the potatoes on?" Kate picked out a cucumber slice and ate it.

"He already did."

"Good. I'm hungry." She picked up the salad dressing and the bowl of vegetables, preparing to carry the items outside. "Can you bring out the paper plates and utensils?"

She never treated Melissa any differently than her son, or so she told herself. She always gave her daughter chores to do so she would feel normal and learn to be independent however she could manage it. Melissa always figured things out. She was resourceful. Kate watched as she put the colorful paper plates and a handful of utensils into a pink basket she kept in the kitchen. Once it was loaded, she hooked it over her arm and picked up her crutches. No problem.

"Got it. Let's go see if dinner is ready." Melissa headed out the side door to the picnic table that sat on the gravel between the house and detached garage. It was a pretty area. Her mom had placed six half-whiskey barrels around and filled them to overflowing with flowers of every color. The pergola her mom had Jed build over the table was nearly covered with pink climbing roses and Morning Glories. It smelled like heaven between the perfume from the blooms and the aroma of food cooking over an open flame.

Melissa set the basket down and then maneuvered onto the bench. The shade cast by the vines overhead created a cool environment, and thanks to her mom planting basil, sage, and lavender in the beds against the house, mosquitoes were not a problem. She reached into the basket and pulled out the plates and a bottled water she'd thrown in. Unscrewing the cap, she took a sip and looked around. Their house sat at the end of a cul-de-sac with a vacant lot on the right. The owner of the property hadn't built anything on it since they'd lived there, and usually Jed cut the grass for them, mostly so it wouldn't look trashy and invite critters like snakes or gators to come hide in the weeds. She was lost in thought when a Toyota truck pulled into the driveway.

Wade saw Melissa immediately. She turned her head and nearly spit out the water she was drinking. The cascade of her hair came down fast like a shield as she hid her face from view. It seemed that Jed hadn't informed her he was coming to dinner. For some odd reason, this made him smile. He turned off the engine and climbed out. Mrs. Ryan came over and hugged him.

"Wade! Did you come for dinner?"

Wade liked Mrs. Ryan a lot. She was like a second mom to him. "I did. Jed called me just as I was getting off work. He saved me from a peanut butter and jelly sandwich."

"Well, good. That isn't dinner. Come on over here. It's almost finished cooking." She led him to the table where Melissa sat, still looking down.

Wade boldly sat right next to her. "Hey. Twice in one day, huh? If I didn't know any better, I'd think you were stalking me or something."

Melissa looked up, surprise written all over her face. "I am not! You're the one who came up to me! Twice." A tinge of anger laced her words. Her embarrassment made her defensive. Wade grinned, and Melissa realized he was only teasing her. "That wasn't nice."

"Maybe, but at least you spoke to me. I swear, it's like I'm a leper or something. Why don't you like me, Melissa?" He nudged her foot with his.

"Who said I didn't like you?"

"Well, whenever I come around, you run and hide. I was beginning to think I must smell bad or something." He watched her face redden and waited for her to speak, to say anything. He had to admit, it was fun goading her.

She rolled her eyes. "You don't smell bad." Again, she hung her head, but Wade could see a hint of a smile. He liked that. A lot.

He leaned close to her ear, sniffing once, and whispered, "You don't smell bad, either."

Melissa felt his warm breath fan her hair and her face caught fire. The blush that spread up her neck and over her cheeks burned.

"So, is my steak ready or what, Ryan?" Wade turned his attention to Jed.

"Coming up, man. Bring some plates over here, would ya?"

Wade got up and carried the paper plates to the grill. Jed began plopping juicy steaks down on each one. Wade carried back three, one for Mrs. Ryan, one for himself, and one for Melissa.

Jed followed behind with hot, foil-wrapped baked potatoes stuck onto the prongs of his barbecue fork. After everyone was served, he joined them with the last, and biggest steak on his own plate.

It was the first time Melissa had eaten around a boy who wasn't her brother, and she was more than aware he was more than just a boy. At twenty-two, Wade was a young man. She had trouble enjoying her dinner. Every bite she took felt like she was shoveling large portions of food into her face even though she'd cut her steak up into small pieces. Usually, she wouldn't have any difficulty polishing off one of Jed's steaks, but with Wade sitting at their little picnic table, right next to her, the idea of him seeing her eat so much was embarrassing. She picked at her salad and took only a few bites of her baked potato.

"What's wrong with your steak, Mel?" Jed stared at her with one eyebrow raised and his fork halfway to his mouth.

"Nothing. Just not very hungry." She muttered the words, then glanced sideways and saw that Wade's lips were twitching. He was laughing at her.

"It must be me. I seem to make Melissa want to run away and now I'm putting her off her food." He turned and winked at her.

"That's not true." Melissa stabbed another bite of steak and ate it to prove him wrong.

"Good. Because you don't strike me as one of those kinds of women who pick at salads for fear a guy would realize she actually does eat."

Jed looked at Wade, then at his sister, and then caught his mother's eye. Mrs. Ryan quickly changed the subject.

"How's that girlfriend of yours, Wade?"

Wade almost choked on his food as Mrs. Ryan subtly reminded him that he shouldn't be teasing her daughter. It was a cold bucket of water, one he knew he deserved, but he rolled with it.

"She's doing all right. Still not happy I'll be leaving at the end of summer."

Mrs. Ryan nodded. "Well, she'll be okay. You're doing the right thing. Having her up in Boston with you would just be a distraction. If it's meant to be, she'll wait."

"I'll keep her company, buddy." Jed wiggled his eyebrows at Wade.

Wade laughed. "You're not her type, Jed."

"Oh, really? And what type is that?"

"Tall, blond, and handsome."

"Boys!" Mrs. Ryan rolled her eyes as her son and his friend began a friendly kick fight under the table. "Stop before you accidentally kick you sister!" She smacked Jed on the back of his head.

Melissa turned and lifted her legs over the bench, preparing to stand.

"Where are you going?" Wade stopped kicking and turned to her.

"To put my plate in the trash." She stood and leaned onto the table, and then loaded the basket with her plate and utensils.

Not wanting to see her run off yet again, Wade got up and began helping her.

"Here, let me get that." He added his own plate to hers, then threw a questioning look at Jed.

"I'm not finished yet. You go ahead." Jed saw his mom about to rise and join them. He pulled her back down by her elbow. She landed hard on her butt, and when she turned to scold her son, he shook his head silently, the look in his eyes saying, "*Stay put.*'

Wade walked with Melissa to the house. Neither said a word. When they disappeared inside, Mrs. Ryan turned quickly to Jed.

"What the heck are you doing? He has a girlfriend. Why are you letting him tease and flirt with your sister like that?" She looked at the kitchen window and saw them both pass by inside. "I thought he was better than that."

"He is better than that. Mom, haven't you noticed? Mel likes him. That's why she runs off every time Wade comes by."

"Well, that doesn't make a lick of sense!"

"Sure, it does. She hasn't had any experience around guys, well, except for me, but I don't count. Wade won't do anything disrespectful. He knows I'd kick his ass, but I think this will be good for her. She's not just shy, mom, she's practically a hermit. Mel needs to gain a little confidence in herself, and if she can feel comfortable opening up a little with Wade, that would be a good thing. Besides, Arlene isn't all that." He chewed a forkful of salad.

"What do you mean?" Mrs. Ryan resumed eating, thinking about her son's words.

"I mean I think she's cheating on him."

"What? What makes you think so?"

"Just some gossip that's been going around. She's really unhappy about Wade getting out of here while she's stuck with nowhere to go. I don't think she's the type who can wait."

"Well, that doesn't mean she's cheating."

Jed sighed. "No. It doesn't mean she's cheating, except that she is. With his cousin, Bart."

Mrs. Ryan dropped her fork into her plate. "The older one? The one who's married?"

"Yeah." Jed sipped his beer.

"You're sure?"

"I'm sure."

"Does Wade have any idea?" She looked toward the house.

"No, and I'm not going to be the one to tell him, either. But that's why I'm okay with him talking to Mel. He's a good guy. He'll do the right thing. It's only talking, and Mel could use the social interaction."

"It's not harmless, Jed. If you're right, and Melissa does like this young man, his attention is only going to stoke that feeling and make it grow. And then what? It goes nowhere because Wade has a girlfriend, whether she's a cheater or not. Your sister will get her feelings hurt." Worry marred her forehead.

Jed chewed his lip thoughtfully. "I know. But mom, it's going to happen to her someday. It may as well happen first with someone who won't treat her badly. You can't protect her from the world forever, you know. She's almost twenty."

Kate Ryan sighed. She didn't like the idea of her daughter getting hurt. If she was going to fall in love with some boy who could love her back, then fine. But if she fell in love with Wade over a few moments of attention—if he didn't return the same feelings, that just didn't seem fair. She didn't like it. But Jed was right. Melissa, despite being encouraged to get out more and have friends, didn't. She stayed close to her and to her brother instead. It really wasn't the best possible life she could imagine for her daughter. And she did like Wade. In her heart, she knew the kid wouldn't harm Melissa. It was just jarring to see him suddenly take any interest in her after coming around for a while now. She'd never seen them even say hello to each other. What in the world had gotten into Wade Walker?

"You didn't have to help, you know. I can handle carrying my own plate." Melissa dumped the plates into the trash can. Wade stood behind her leaning against the counter.

"I know that." He watched her shake the basket and then turn to rinse it out in the sink.

"How would you know that?" She glanced at him sideways, slightly annoyed.

"Because Jed says you're stubborn as a mule and twice as independent."

"Jed shouldn't be talking about me to his friends." She turned off the water and dried her hands on the towel.

"I don't know, he's awfully proud of you." Wade stuck his hands in his pockets and crossed one foot over the other.

Melissa didn't know what to say to that.

"He says you're, like, a professional photographer."

The corner of her lip lifted at that. "Not a professional. I just really like taking pictures, and I've sold some."

"Sounds like a professional to me. Maybe you'll show me sometime?"

Melissa looked at Wade. She was trying to decide if he was seriously interested or just being nice. Other than her family and the sites that had purchased her work, she'd never shown her photographs to anyone. They were personal, an extension of herself. He held her gaze, and for the life of her, she couldn't look away. The slight smile tugging the corners of his lips made her blush. The tension in the air between them sizzled with awareness, an awareness she didn't know how to handle or what to do with it.

Wade leaned closer, his eyes never leaving hers. "Are you thinking about saying yes?"

Melissa felt the full force of his presence and leaned backward. As she did, her crutch slipped from her hand, and she listed sideways onto her weaker right leg. Quick as lightning, Wade reached out and wrapped his arms around her, stopping the fall. She found herself held tightly to his chest, his face only inches away from her own.

"Melissa, all you had to do was say yes. No need to fall for me, too." His whispered words were tinged with humor.

Confused and embarrassed, she put her hand on his chest to create some space. "You don't have to tease me, you know."

Wade saw the hurt in her eyes. He realized then she wasn't used to someone flirting with her. He helped her gain her balance but didn't let go of the hold he had on her just yet. His expression turned serious.

"I didn't mean anything by it. It's just hard not to flirt with you. You're so pretty."

Shock replaced her confusion and hurt. She lowered her eyes and let her hair slide forward, hiding her face. Wade reached out to tuck the sleek strands behind her ear, and then gently cupped her face urging her to look up.

"Hasn't anyone ever told you?" His thumb caressed her cheek.

"No." That one word was spoken so low, he almost didn't hear it. He searched her eyes and saw only honesty. She seemed so fragile, like the wrong words would break her.

"Well, I'll be…" Going silent, he let his gaze roam over her face, wonder in his green eyes.

Finally, she couldn't take it anymore. "What?"

He smiled. "I'm the first guy to tell you how beautiful you are. That's kind of special."

Melissa swallowed. First, he'd called her pretty, and now he was saying she was beautiful. She didn't know how to respond. She just stood there with her mouth open, her lips forming a surprised 'O'.

Wade noticed, and his eyes dropped to her lips. Soft, naturally pink, and free of any lipstick. Without any doubt, he knew she'd never been kissed. The temptation to add another first to her list pulled him closer. Their noses touched and he turned his head slightly, angling closer. The space of a single breath separated them. Wade sank his fingers into her hair, gently holding her still. He'd never wanted to kiss anyone in his life as much as he wanted to kiss Melissa Ryan at this moment.

Melissa thought she might faint if she didn't take a breath soon. She felt hot all over. Her heart was racing. She could almost hear the hum between their bodies. *Oh, my God! This is torture. Why would anyone want to do this? Back up! No, come closer. I don't know what to do!* All these thoughts ran through her mind at the speed of light, and while she tried to make sense out of it all, his lips found hers, and the world exploded, ceasing to exist outside of the two of them.

The kiss began as a gentle pressure, a tentative introduction. One, two, and then three soft kisses landed upon her lips like the wings of butterflies. Then Wade kissed her again, his lips sliding across hers, causing a delicate and highly sensitive friction that built upon itself until she sighed. The moment Melissa relaxed, Wade swooped in to deepen the kiss. His tongue ran along her lower lip, dipped inside, and touched hers. As soon as the contact was made, her body came to life. Every part of her was hot and needy. Where she'd felt he was too close before, now he was not close enough. His hands slid down her neck and shoulders roaming over her back and bringing her up against him in a way that made her whole body melt. It was wonderful. It was terrifying, too, because she felt so many things at once, she didn't know what to do or how to react. All she could do was allow herself to be swept along on this current of desire.

Wade got lost in the wonder that was Melissa. What she lacked in experience, she made up for ten times over in passion and enthusiasm. His body responded to her softness, and there was a primal feeling that she was his, all his, and no one had ever kissed her before this day. He would always be her first kiss. Then he realized he'd be yet another first if he didn't stop. He remembered that Jed and Mrs. Ryan were right outside, and he pulled away. They stood, gasping for breath, and staring at each other, stunned. Both surprised, but neither more so than Wade who suddenly recalled he still had a girlfriend.

"I'm sorry. Geez, Melissa, I'm so sorry. I shouldn't have." He backed away and leaned down to pick her crutch up off the floor. He put it in her hand, and turned away, practically running outside. He left her standing in the kitchen, speechless, and now, more confused than ever.

Embarrassment quickly replaced her confusion, and she retreated to her bedroom as fast as she could manage where she slammed the door and shut everyone out. She sat down hard on the edge of her bed. Tears welled up out of nowhere and began to fall. Wade Walker, the guy she'd secretly been crushing on for months had just kissed her senseless in the kitchen, and it was everything she'd ever hoped it would be, but then he'd pushed her away and ran off like she was the most hideous creature in the world. Of course it was all a mistake. Who in his right mind would ever want to kiss her? He'd just been playing with her, and it got out of hand. He never meant it, never meant to kiss her...did he?

She didn't know, and her inexperience with such matters wasn't helping. All she knew was he'd said some nice things, and then kissed her, but then ran away like she was the very devil. Well, Wade Walker could just go jump in a lake as far as she was concerned. She wasn't going to let him play with her like this. He had a girlfriend, a pretty one with legs that worked. Why he'd messed with her was beyond comprehension, but she wasn't going to be the butt of some guy's joke. She heard his truck rev as he pulled out of the driveway. Melissa grabbed her pillow and hugged it tightly to her chest. The pain of rejection was as sharp as a knife to the heart. The tears continued to fall, and she didn't know how to make them stop.

Chapter 3

The familiar rumble of an engine reached Arlene Richard's ear. She pushed hard against the naked chest that she'd been glued to moments earlier and got up.

"You have to go. Hurry!" She tossed pants and a shirt at the man in her bed. As she threw on her clothes, hastily discarded only an hour before, she tossed an irritated glare over her shoulder. "Move faster!" She picked up his shoes and socks and yanked his arm propelling him out of the bedroom and down the hall toward the back door.

He stalled; one bare foot still planted inside. "When will I see you again?" Blue eyes implored her to make another date, and soon!

"I don't know. Get out of here. If Wade finds you here, it's all over. He'll kill you!" She shoved his shoes and socks at him.

Jealousy flashed in Bart Walker's eyes. "I don't give a damn, Arlene. You know as well as I do once he leaves for Boston, he ain't coming back. And you're mine!" He snaked an arm around her waist and pulled her hard against him. He crushed her lips with his own trying to assert dominance. Arlene twisted and punched his shoulders, pushing him off.

"I'm not yours, Bart! You're married. This isn't anything except fun, and the fun's over. Get out!" She slammed the door narrowly missing his foot as he extracted it.

Arlene ran her fingers through her long, blonde hair and pulled it up into a twist. She secured it with a clip as the doorbell rang. She smiled as she swung the door wide.

"Wade!"

Wade leaned on the door jamb and looked at Arlene, taking in her rumpled appearance. "Were you taking a nap?" His teasing smile twitched at the corners of his lips.

"Wade Walker, what are you trying to say?" She put her arms around his neck.

He tucked a curl behind her ear. "You look a little mussed. You're only supposed to look like this after I've made passionate love to you."

Arlene laughed, the sound high and nervous. She gave him a quick kiss and pulled him inside. "You're just being silly. What's going on?"

"I came to see if you wanted to go out to eat since I'm off this afternoon." He followed her into the living room.

"That would be perfect. I'm starving! But I need to shower and get ready. Do you mind waiting?" She stood with her hands on her hips throwing him the supermodel pout.

Wade sighed, then looked at his watch. She got the hint.

"I'll be quick! Thirty minutes, I swear." She zipped off to the bathroom and shut the door.

Wade heard the water running and pulled out his phone, checking for messages. He knew it would be at least an hour no matter what she said. He wandered into her room thinking to grab a short snooze while she did what all women do, take forever. As he entered, he noticed her bed was unmade.

"Getting lazy, Arlene." He muttered the words as he sat on the edge and laid back. An off smell tickled his nose. It wasn't her perfume, but more of a masculine scent. Wrinkling his brow, Wade turned his head to the pillow and sniffed. It was definitely cologne. Strong, cheap cologne. He got up and looked down at the sheets. Something wasn't right. He got closer to the center of the bed and sniffed cautiously. He knew that smell. It was sex. Sex and sweat mingled with someone else's cologne. He jumped back and stood staring at the bed. Arlene began singing offkey in the shower. He checked the floor around the bed but found nothing except her shoes. Then, he got down on the floor and peeked under the bed skirt, sure he'd find some naked fellow beneath. But there were only dust bunnies. Now he just felt foolish.

Rising, he stood looking from the messy bed toward the hallway where the bathroom was located. The odor wafted, teasing him. When he turned, something shiny caught his eye. Next to the wastepaper basket was a wrapper. He picked it up and stared at it. It was a condom wrapper.

"Son of a—"

"Wade? Who're you talking to?" Arlene called from the bathroom.

Terrible thoughts exploded in Wade's head all at once. He knew now that he'd just interrupted his girlfriend having sex with someone, but who? His fists clenched at his sides as he glared a hole through the bathroom door. He tossed the wrapper on the mussed sheets, walked out of the room, and left the house.

Hearing the front door slam, Arlene called out. "Wade? Wade?" She shut off the water and stepped out, grabbing a towel, and wrapping it around her wet body. She looked out into the hall. "Wade? Are you here?"

Silence.

She stepped into the living room and looked out the window. Wade's truck was gone. Confused, she wandered back to her bedroom and stopped dead in her tracks. In the middle of her bed sat a gold Magnum wrapper.

"Oh, crap!"

Wade sped through the streets, white knuckling the steering wheel. He didn't know where he was going. All he knew was that he needed some space, needed to be away from Arlene, so he could think. She was cheating on him. His girlfriend was cheating on him. But with who? He just couldn't wrap his mind around it all. They had plans, plans that had been made back in high school when they first started dating.

She was the only girl he'd been serious about. Sure, there had been a couple other girls before her, his first kiss, known as Sarah Henry, and his first 'time' which was with Mary Ellen Bennett, but Arlene was different from the rest. He was her first lover, and she was his first love. He passed Big Boy's Burgers and turned right. Before he realized it, he was near the far edge of Pelican's Cove. This stretch of beach was shaped like a seashell and surrounded by high cliffs. Large boulders jutted up from the water further out creating a barrier. It was great for swimming because boats couldn't navigate through all the rocks. The open spaces between the high peaks were dangerous because more jagged rocks were right beneath the surface of the waves. It was a peaceful place to be, which suited him right now.

He noticed a truck parked close to the road but didn't pay any attention to it. He pulled further out and onto the sand. There, he parked, turning off the engine and rolling down the windows. He stared out at the water. The sun was low in the sky. It would set soon, and the cove would be almost pitch black except for the light cast by the moon. The sound of rolling waves had a calming effect. His anger cooled, and he began to wonder just what he'd done to send Arlene into the arms of another guy. Could it be she really couldn't wait for him? Was his going off to earn his law degree really too much to bear?

He thought about his own actions the other night at Jed's. He'd kissed Melissa Ryan. Melissa was not his girlfriend, which made what he did worse, and certainly not fair to her or to his relationship with Arlene. Was his own action any different than hers?

He wasn't sorry about the kiss. The kiss was great. In fact, something about it, about Melissa, struck him in a way he'd never felt before, not even with Arlene. Kissing Arlene was like getting to kiss a supermodel.

She was perfect, beautiful. Every guy who laid eyes on her wished he was dating her. But kissing Melissa felt like she was made just for him. Like they were always meant to kiss only each other. Except for the fact that he wasn't free to kiss her, he wasn't sorry at all. His introspection was interrupted by a movement out of the corner of his eye. He turned and looked off to the left. There, scrambling down a ledge on the cliff was the very person he'd been thinking about. Melissa Ryan had her camera around her neck and was slowly making her way off the massive rock. Her hands hung on for dear life and her left foot tried to gain purchase. Her crutches were waiting on the sand below. She still had at least ten feet to descend, and it looked like she was about to drop. Wade's heart pounded as fear flooded his body. He got out of his car and began to run in her direction.

"Melissa, wait! Don't move!" His sneakered feet pounded the sand.

Melissa heard her name and glanced over her shoulder. Her hand slipped, and her foot missed its hold. She plummeted down the rock and landed hard on the ground.

Wade's heart stopped. He bounded the last few yards and slid down next to her. Gently, he touched Melissa's face, placing his hands on her cheeks.

"Melissa, are you okay? Oh, my God. Please tell me you're all right?" He inspected her from head to toe. She was sprawled on her back, her face scrunched up into a painful grimace. "Where does it hurt?" He ran his hands down her arms, her legs, and then her sides. "I don't see anything out of place. Where's the pain? Are you breathing?" He leaned down and stared at her face, anxious and full of worry.

Melissa exhaled. "Ow!" she yelled.

Wade cringed, sure she'd broken a bone. "What hurts?"

She opened one eye and then the other and looked at him. His face hovered above her.

"My pride," she muttered. A tear trickled down her cheek.

"That's not pride causing this." He wiped it away with his thumb.

"No, but I got the wind knocked out of me and landed on my butt." She sniffed, looking away as heat climbed her cheeks. Adrenaline rushed through her body, causing her to tremble.

"I'm sorry. I shouldn't have startled you, but when I saw you up on that rock, I damn near had a stroke." Wade settled down by her side, afraid to move her. Instead, he slipped his arm beneath her head and held her. "Dammit, Melissa, what are you doing out here climbing rocks by yourself?"

"I was just taking some pictures. I come out here by myself all the time. I don't need a babysitter." She tried to move, but Wade clamped his other arm around her waist and held her still.

"Don't move. Just rest for a moment. That was quite a fall." He was leaning on his elbow looking down into her face. Anyone passing by would think they were two lovers on the beach.

"What are you doing here?" She eyed him suspiciously.

He sighed. "I came out here to think."

"About what?"

Wade wasn't sure he wanted to talk about Arlene's cheating with anyone, let alone Melissa, but he didn't want to lie to her, either. "About my relationship with Arlene." He left it at that.

Melissa searched his face. He wasn't telling her everything, she could tell. Whatever it was, it was serious enough to send him out to this secluded cove to think it over. "So did you?"

Wade brushed sand out of her hair. "Did I what?"

"Think about it?" She felt his fingers tangle into her hair and gently shake out the grains. He continued winding a strand around his finger, over and over again. The action sent tingles over her scalp and down her back.

"No. Not really. I haven't been here very long. Then I saw you, and you're all I've thought about since."

His honesty was like a warm caress. It took away her annoyance and cooled the residual anger she felt toward him for running away after he kissed her the other night.

"I'm sorry." Her softly spoken words drifted up to his ears.

"I'm not." He watched her, his eyes taking in every curve and angle from the smooth skin of her cheeks to the soft lilt of her lips. Finally, he let his gaze travel to her big, brown eyes. He tried counting her eyelashes, but there were too many. All the while his fingers wound through her hair.

The air grew thick with sizzling awareness.

"I think I'm okay now." She pushed past him to sit up.

Wade let her go but stayed where he was. He dusted more sand off her back, then settled into an open hand rubbing motion.

Melissa looked over her shoulder. "You don't have to do that, you know." She noticed he was still touching her. She didn't know why he kept doing it, but she suspected he felt sorry for her.

"I know. But I want to. Kinda can't seem to help myself." He sat up, his face level once again with hers. "I like touching you, Melissa."

Her breath caught in her throat.

Wade moved closer. "And I liked kissing you, too. More than I can say." His eyes dropped to her lips which were now parted in surprise. He inched closer, his hand sliding around her neck, gently pulling her in.

"Then why did you run off?" Her question splashed cold water all over his intentions.

He smiled wryly. "Because, I shouldn't have been kissing you. It wasn't fair to you."

"Because of Arlene?" Melissa waited.

"Yeah, because of her. And because you deserve so much more than that."

"Then why are you about to kiss me again?" Her eyes beseeched him, wide with hurt and apprehension.

Wade caressed her cheek with his thumb. He knew with certainty he should not lie to her. He knew how it felt to be lied to, after all.

"Because I like you, and when I'm near you, I want to be as close to you as possible. I want so badly to kiss you. I don't even know how to explain it, really."

His admission hit Melissa like an arrow aimed straight at her heart. Cupid's arrow. "I like you, too."

Her shy admission caused a cocky smile to spread across his handsome face.

Seeing that smile, Melissa bit her lip, unsure now what to do or say. She felt naked, vulnerable.

"Don't look at me like that, Wade." She turned her head away seeking to break the eye contact that had her feeling hot and nervous again.

"Like what?" Amusement tinged his words.

"Like you want to kiss me." The air around them sizzled. She thought she might not ever be able to breathe properly again if he didn't do something, like back up...or move closer.

"I do. I do want to kiss you, Melissa, more than I want anything else in this world right now." His deep voice vibrated with a raw passion that flavored his words. They tasted like the sweetest wine as his lips crushed hers stealing her breath and firing her blood.

This wasn't like their first kiss. It wasn't hesitant. It didn't wait. Instead, it consumed them both. The glide of lips caressing as tongues entwined, danced, and laid claim sparked a fire that blazed between them. Wade laid Melissa down onto the sand pillowing her head with one hand while the other ran down her side and settled on her hip. He pulled her against him and slid his blue-jeaned leg between hers. His fingers caressed her thigh while his kisses robbed her of all thought.

Melissa was burning with desire. It was all so new and it made her dizzy. Her body was hot and needy. She didn't know what to do about it, but kissing Wade helped. She reveled in the taste and scent of him. His touch sent tingles skittering over her body, and they all settled low in her belly. She'd never felt like this before, but she liked it. She liked Wade. She thought she might even love him. Tentatively, she let her hands wander over his broad shoulders and down his strong arms. As she grew more confident, her hands roamed lower, and her fingers slipped beneath his T-shirt to draw circles on the warm skin of his lower back. He responded by pressing his hips against hers. The friction was delicious, and she did it again, experimenting with her own power to move him. His lips trailed along her jaw and down to her neck. There, he licked the sensitive skin below her ear and nibbled a path to her shoulder.

Melissa arched her back, and his head dropped lower, skimming the neckline of her blouse. His hand glided up her ribcage, and in a stealthy move, reached for second base. Shocked at the firestorm his warm palm ignited, she pushed at him. It was too much too fast.

"Wade. Wade, stop!" She placed both hands on his shoulders and shoved.

He pulled up to his elbows and looked down at her, passion making his green eyes glow. "What's wrong?"

Melissa took three deep breaths. "You're going too fast. I'm not ready.... I...I just can't." She rambled, unable to express all that was going on inside her head or her body.

Wade bit his lip trying not to smile. He lowered his head as he slid down her body and laid his cheek on her stomach. He gave her some room to breathe but couldn't make himself break away completely. Instead, he remained still inhaling her warm, sexy scent while staring out at the water. The sun was nearly below the horizon.

Melissa looked down at the top of his head in wonder. Her fingers slipped into his dark-blond strands exhibiting a mind of their own. They played there while she turned and watched the sun set. It was peaceful, and the breeze was turning cooler, but she felt warm and safe. She just didn't know what to do about it all. This was her first time making out with a guy, and it wasn't just any guy, it was Wade Walker. And he wasn't hers.

Wade concentrated on breathing. His body felt tight and uncomfortable, and only time would take care of that. His passion cooled, but his feelings for Melissa grew exponentially. The way he felt just laying here with her was better than any other time with Arlene, and he didn't know what to make of that. He was no better than her after all. Or maybe it was just time to move on. He didn't know, but he knew now he didn't want to lose Melissa. He had to make things right, clear the path. Melissa Ryan deserved a boyfriend who was all in, not halfway.

"You okay?" he asked.

"Yes." She continued watching the last rays dip below the horizon. The sun faded, and then dropped out of sight.

"Good." He caressed her arm. "Melissa?"

She felt the rumble of his deep voice like a swarm of fuzzy bees over her tummy. The tingles that this caused were both terrifying and exciting.

"Uh huh?"

He turned his head, resting his chin on her stomach, and gazed up at her face. "I'm going to make this right."

She raised one eyebrow. "What do you mean?"

He took her hand in his and kissed her fingers. "I mean that I'm going to fix this mess. I want you, Melissa. I want you to be my girl." He arose and moved over her, bringing his face level with hers. "Will you be my girl, Melissa Ryan?"

And just like that, Melissa felt hot and bothered all over again. "What about Arlene?"

"That's why I was up here today. That's what I was thinking about. It's over. We're finished." He didn't add any details.

"But you two have been together for a long time. Are you sure?" Melissa couldn't believe what she was hearing. It was like a dream.

He ran a finger over her lips causing sparks to ignite. "I'm sure. Ever since you finally spoke to me, I haven't been able to stop thinking about you. I like you, Melissa. I like everything about you. It's like I've always known you."

Melissa smiled. Her heart raced like a wild filly running free. He was hers. He said so. All she had to do was say yes. Shyness overcame her but she fought through it, boldly reaching for happiness.

"Then...yes."

Wade grinned, joy glowing in his green eyes, and then kissed her senseless. Again. This time, there was no guilt.

Chapter 4

Wade wiped his hands on his blue jeans. His palms were sweating revealing how anxious he was over what he was about to do. It wasn't going to be easy. He was still mad, but part of him knew that this was the way it was supposed to go. He pushed the doorbell and stepped back.

Arlene opened the door and when she saw Wade standing there, paused, unsure what to say. Her eyes were red rimmed, as if she'd been crying since he ran off yesterday. Her face was bare of makeup, and she wore his old button-down jean shirt over a tank top and a pair of shorts. He remembered the day she'd hijacked it from his closet. She told him that wearing it made her feel like he still had his arms around her when he wasn't with her. After he said what he came to say, it would be all she had left…that, and whoever it was with whom she was cheating on him.

"Hey." She crossed her arms over her chest and waited.

"Hey." Wade took a deep breath. "I just came by to say this in person."

She looked up, dread in her big blue eyes. "Say what?"

"It's over, Arlene. I'm not even going to ask who the hell it is you're screwing. It doesn't matter. It just doesn't because it's a deal breaker. No need trying to deny it, either." He held up his hand when he saw her about to object. "The only thing I want to know is why? Why would you do this to me? I mean, if you weren't happy, why not just say so and break up first before getting with someone else? I figure I've earned at least that much respect."

Arlene's eyes filled with tears. She sniffed. "I don't know why, Wade. I guess I was just scared that you wouldn't come back once you left. It was an option, and I...I liked the attention."

That hit him like a slap.

"I didn't give you enough attention? I gave you all my attention from the moment we met. I planned my entire life around you, Arlene! Around us!"

She cringed at the anger in his voice.

"I'm sorry, Wade. Please. Please don't break up with me!" She threw her arms around his neck. "I love you." She kept repeating those three words, her face buried in his shoulder as she clung to him.

Wade reached up and gently pried her from his person. As he turned his face above her hair, the faint scent of cologne hit him. He pushed her back violently.

"Were you with him again today?" he asked, incredulous.

She looked surprised. "What? No, I...I mean..." She stopped, confused. "How?" she finally asked.

"I can smell his cologne. It was all over your bed sheets yesterday, and it's all over you today. Some jerk who wears more cologne than a pimp. That's who you choose to be with? Christ, Arlene!" Wade turned and walked away. Halfway to his car, he looked back. "I hate myself for asking, but who is he?" He stood waiting.

Arlene was crying outright now. "I don't want to say."

"It's someone I know?" The shock of betrayal lit Wade's eyes.

She remained silent. He could see she wasn't going to give him an answer, but he knew one thing; he'd know eventually. And when he found out, he planned on pummeling whoever it was into the dirt on principle alone.

He got into his truck and with one last look at the girl he'd planned to marry, he put it in reverse and pulled away. His last image of Arlene Richards was of a broken young woman standing on her porch crying her eyes out, wearing his shirt, and drenched in the cheap scent of another man. He felt bad, terrible and torn and betrayed, but he also felt free. She was his first love, and that was significant. He just wished it had ended better. He hated that she cheated on him. He hated that they had to go through that. He even hated that he wasn't anywhere near as upset about it as she was, and he knew that was all because of Melissa Ryan. He wanted to see her but going over there right after breaking up with Arlene seemed somehow wholly disrespectful to both. He headed home. He needed time. Tomorrow was a new day, and his new life with Melissa would begin. It was a clean slate. They'd take it slow, and really work on becoming friends. Of course, there would be kissing, lots of kissing, but he didn't want to rush. She was still Jed's sister, and that alone made her deserve his very best. Jed was his friend, and messing with a friend's sister was never something any guy did unless he was one hundred percent serious about her. Before he could even take Melissa out on their first official date, he knew he needed to get Jed's blessing.

Jed stood stock still in his living room above the garage staring down at Wade, who sat on the edge of the couch. He looked nervous. Jed could almost see the sweat trying to pop out on his forehead. He squinted at him, and waited a good, long time before speaking.

"Did you just ask me if you could date my sister?"

Wade nodded. He knew there was more that he would have to explain before it was all said and done.

"Aren't you already dating someone else?" Jed pushed his fist into his hand, his mind running ninety miles a minute. He knew Arlene was cheating on Wade. He knew his sister liked him. He'd figured that one out a while back. But he was surprised to see his friend sitting in his home asking for his blessing to date Melissa. He didn't have the whole story, but he knew there was a story. A juicy one.

"I was." Wade evaded a more detailed answer. Still, he knew Jed would pull it out of him. This was going to be like getting a tooth pulled out by a sadistic dentist wielding a rusty pair of pliers.

"Was. As in, not anymore?" Jed crossed his arms over his chest.

"That's right. Not anymore." The standoff continued.

"Since when?" Jed cocked his head as his eyes bored into Wade's.

"Since yesterday." Wade felt a bead of sweat trickle down his forehead. He wondered if Jed made it hot in the house on purpose.

"So, as of yesterday, out of the blue, you and Arlene Richards, your girlfriend—nay—fiancé of the past couple of years, are suddenly no longer a couple?"

Wade sighed. "Yes."

Jed began to pace, taking on all the mannerisms of a courtroom prosecutor. "And the very next day you're asking to date *my* sister?"

"That's right." Wade reached up to wipe his forehead with the back of his hand.

"What makes you think you're good enough for my sister?"

That got Wade's attention. "What? You know me, Jed. I'm not a bad guy."

Jed spun around to change direction and hide the laugh that threatened to erupt. He composed himself before he faced his friend again.

"I don't know, man. I mean, you just broke up with your long-time girlfriend yesterday, and now you want to date Melissa. What does that say about you? You barely know her. What if she doesn't want to date you?"

"She does." Wade answered before thinking, and then bit his tongue.

Jed stopped pacing. "How do you know that?" His dark eyebrow rose, and he stared hard at Wade. Usually, this was Jed's best Dwayne 'The Rock" Johnson imitation, but today, it was all Jed Ryan.

"I just know." Wade didn't want to reveal anything that might embarrass her.

"You just know…based on talking to her, what? Twice? Three times?"

Wade rubbed his hands on his legs and stood up. "Look, Jed. I know it sounds crazy. I get it. If she were my sister and you were asking this, I'd be skeptical too." He paused. "Something happened with Arlene. I don't really want to go into details, but it was bad, bad enough to break us up. Even so, I think it was longer in coming than I realized. And, well, as far as your sister goes, she's special." He looked down. "Ever since I first spoke to her, I knew that. Yeah, you've said so yourself a hundred times," he said, gesturing wildly, "but until she looked at me and recognized I was alive, I had no idea just how amazing she was." He looked Jed in the eye. "I really like her. I'd like very much to take her out on a date and see if there's more there, respectfully, of course. I'd never do anything to hurt her."

Jed watched his friend sweat a little longer. A full minute ticked by. Finally, a smile spread across his face, and he reached out a hand. "Okay."

Wade looked surprised. "Okay?"

"Yeah, okay. You can take Melissa out on a date…if she'll have you."

Wade grasped Jed's hand and shook. They leaned in for the bro half-hug/back slap combo. "Thanks, man. It means a lot to me."

Jed, still grasping Wade's hand tight, grew serious. "It should go without saying that if you do hurt her in any way, I'll have to beat your ass."

"And I'd deserve it. No worries."

They came to an agreement and let go. Jed laughed. "Well, now that I've made you piss your pants, you want a beer?"

"Jackass." Wade exhaled. "And yes!"

After spending an hour with Jed, Wade made his way downstairs to the house. Melissa had been out earlier, which suited his purpose since he wanted to get Jed's blessing, but he heard her truck pull up, and not more than ten minutes later, his friend thankfully cut him loose.

"Go. I can see I lost you already. Geez." Jed waved Wade off and went back to his video game, solo this time. He smiled the moment the door closed, shaking his head.

When Wade reached the house, he didn't even knock. He just walked into the kitchen and gave Mrs. Ryan a quick greeting and a hug before making a beeline for Melissa's room.

Kate Ryan stood looking toward the hallway leading to the bedrooms with a surprised look on her face.

In her room, Melissa set her camera down on the bed and reached for her laptop. She logged in, plugged the cable into her camera, and waited for the images to download. Several from the day before began to pop up on screen as one after the other completed loading. They were all taken before her fall off the rock ledge. The deep blue green of the cove triggered the memory of Wade's kiss. She closed her eyes and let her mind drift back. She could still feel the warmth of his hands checking her for injury, hear the concern in his voice, and taste the sweetness of his lips. The mattress dipped behind her, and strong arms slipped around her waist.

"What are you daydreaming about?" The tickle of Wade's breath on her ear combined with his sudden appearance in her room startled Melissa.

"What are you doing here?" She turned and was immediately captivated by the twinkle in his green eyes.

"I'm here to see my girlfriend." He dropped a quick kiss on her lips.

Melissa smiled. "So, I'm officially your girlfriend now?"

"You are."

"My family is going to be a little freaked out." She chewed her lip. She'd never had a boyfriend before. She had no clue how to proceed and felt self-conscious about it.

"Jed already knows. I got his blessing earlier while you were out. And I'm pretty sure your mom knows by now, too."

"You asked Jed's permission?" She laughed to hide her embarrassment. It sounded absurd, old-fashioned, and kind of sweet.

"He put me through the wringer, but I think he just did that for his own sick amusement. He seems okay with it."

Melissa laid her palm against his cheek, her eyes full of concern. "And how did the rest of it go?"

He knew she meant Arlene. He covered her hand with his own. "As expected. But it's over. Done. I'd rather talk about us." He looked down at her computer screen. "What have you got there?"

Melissa set the computer on the bed between them. "I was trying to get some images for a travel website. They wanted specific locations on the Florida coast."

"So how much do they pay for these photos?"

She began to filter through them one by one as he watched. "It depends on the client. But for these, they're offering $150 each for professional shots. I'm not really a professional, but they seem to like my work."

Wade raised an eyebrow. "If someone is paying you that much for a photograph, then you're a professional. Make no mistake." He lifted her hand and kissed her fingers. "How many images do they need?"

"Ten." She closed the computer.

Wade blew out a breath. "Wow! You make over a grand per job? Come here, sugar mama!" He pulled her close and she laughed. When his lips claimed hers, she melted.

Melissa couldn't believe this was happening. She had a budding career, and now she had Wade Walker. She was truly happy, and right at this moment, hot and oddly achy as his hands slid over her back and his tongue caressed hers. How could she be so lucky as to find a guy who could like her despite her disability? She mentally slapped her pessimistic self and melted into his kiss.

Chapter 5

A month passed. It was the best month of Melissa's life. She and Wade went on their first date, the traditional dinner and a movie. For their second date, he arranged for a coastal boat tour. It was a little corny for Florida natives, but it turned out playing tourist was fun. She brought her camera and took several pictures of dolphins and rays jumping out of the ocean. However, her favorite pictures from that day were the selfies they took together. In one, Wade grabbed her chin and kissed her just as the shutter released. She framed that one and kept it by her bedside. What really surprised her were the images she didn't know were on the camera. Apparently, when she set it down to reach over the side and pet the bottlenose that chirped joyfully at her, he'd snapped a few pictures of his own. She saw herself through his eyes, smiling, hair pulled back in a ponytail flying in the breeze, and stroking the rubbery wet nose of a curious sea mammal. Another was close up. She was laughing hysterically when that same dolphin splashed her with his tail, drops of salty spray catching the sun and filtering rainbows around her.

She'd printed that one out and gave it to him as a present.

That moment was now forever etched in Wade's memory. He'd unwrapped the blue paper. Inside was a silver frame showcasing Melissa's smiling face. He loved it. And he loved her. He knew if he didn't tell her soon, he might accidentally blurt it out at some weird moment in front of everyone. Their third official date was coming up on Friday. He hadn't counted all the time spent together hanging out at her house with Jed and her mom watching movies, barbecuing, or even when he helped Jed plant two new crepe myrtle trees in the yard while Mrs. Ryan served iced tea, and Melissa took mock 'calendar boy' photos of him and her brother posing with shovels and flexing their biceps. Those were good times, but he liked the quiet moments, like right now.

They sat outside beneath the stars and talked about whatever popped into their heads. Wade told her about his dream to become a finance attorney, but that he was also interested in advocating for the environment and wanted to get other like-minded people to form a non-profit that focused on protecting the coastlines from pollution.

"Our oceans are just full of plastics and toxins. It's killing the marine life, and the birds eat the plastic caps because they don't know any difference between them and a small fish. They're dying at unprecedented rates. It may mean I might need to have some kind of concentration in environmental law. I don't know. I guess I'll find my way through it when I get there."

"Why not just go straight into environmental law?" Melissa looked up at him from her comfortable spot lying on his shoulder.

"My dad would freak. He's always saying, *'Think about the future, boy. There's no future in being a hippie!'* I disagree, but he's helping pay for my first year. I don't think he understands that there's no future without a healthy ocean, but he's older and comes from a generation that didn't have to worry about this stuff. So, unless I suddenly hit the lottery, I feel like I have to respect his wishes. If he's helping pay for it, he has a say in which direction I go."

"Can't you take some extra classes on your own then?"

Wade looked down at her and kissed her forehead. "Yes, Miss Smartie-Pants. I can. I probably will, but it would be during the summers."

She thought about what that meant. "How long will it take to finish?"

He ran his fingers through her hair, thoughtful. "Well, that depends on passing all the classes, but in all, two to three years."

"Oh," she said, looking down.

Wade smiled. "I hear they have some really beautiful places to photograph up in Boston. It's an historic city, you know. Boston Tea Party, Colonial era, old streetcars, and the homes of famous people like Nathanial Hawthorne."

Melissa sat up. "Well, that's all well and good, but I'll be here, and you'll be there."

Wade leaned forward and wrapped his arms around her. "Maybe I didn't make myself clear, Miss Ryan. I'm saying that I'd like it a lot if you'd come up to Boston every summer and stay with me. There's no reason why we should wait that long to be together. I know I'll be busy during the semesters, but summer, well, even with one or two classes, would just be lonely as hell without you."

Melissa's eyes widened in surprise. "You want me to come stay with you?"

"Yes." He tucked a strand of her silky brown hair behind her ear. "Will you?"

She thought about it. She'd never lived anywhere but north Florida. Boston seemed almost like another planet; one she could explore with Wade by her side.

She smiled. "Yes. Yes, I'll come stay with you, but only if you really want me to. I mean, I don't want to be in the way or anything."

Wade let out a whoop and scooped her up onto his lap. "I really, really want you to." He kissed her quickly. "And thank you."

She giggled. "For what?"

"For making me so damn happy." His lips claimed hers again, slower this time, and with a tenderness that made her heart swell with love.

Friday night arrived amid a storm warning. Melissa watched the red ticker move across the bottom of the television screen as the weatherman from their local station warned of strong thunderstorms. She made a last-minute decision to twist her hair up. All the humidity would just make it frizz and curl, and she'd be worrying about it all night.

Wade wouldn't tell her where they were going. He said it was a surprise, so she really didn't know what to wear. She didn't usually wear dresses, but the dark fuchsia straight skirt with matching tank top felt casual while looking dressy. She slipped into wedged silver-strapped sandals and accessorized with silver jewelry. By now, she felt comfortable with Wade, and the self-consciousness that had plagued her early on over her crutches dissipated. The only time he seemed to notice them was when he instinctively reached out to help her transition in and out of their vehicles. Other than that, it was like they weren't even there.

"So, stay in tonight. If you have to be out, leave early and go slowly. Avoid low water crossings. Remember, don't drown, turn around!" The weatherman signed off, and the sports anchor began his spiel. Melissa tuned him out. She pushed the last pin into place and sat back viewing her handiwork. Her updo was elegant, probably more so than the occasion required, but she felt pretty. Her phone vibrated on the vanity. She looked down and saw it was a text message from Wade.

On my way to pick up the most perfect girl in the world. You might know her. She's beautiful, sweet, makes me happy, and it's our third date! Figured it out yet? (winking emoji) I'm the luckiest guy in the world. I'd wait a lifetime for you, Melissa Ryan, but I'm excited to say I only have to wait twenty more minutes to have you in my arms. Ready for me, babe? Here I come!

Melissa laughed as she wiped a tear from her eye. She clicked SAVE on her messages. This was by far the sweetest message Wade had sent her, and he'd been sending some good ones. After he said goodnight last Tuesday, she received a message that made her grip her sheets as she lay in bed. *Thinking of you, about kissing you. I can still smell the scent of your hair on my hands, and all I can think about is that sound you made when I nibbled your ear. God, Melissa, you're so sexy. I don't think I'm going to get to sleep any time soon! Yours, Wade.*

She knew things were getting heated between them. All she had to do was picture his smile and she went all warm and gooey inside. She really didn't know what to expect from tonight's date, but just in case, she'd gone all out in getting ready. It might just be *'the night'*. Melissa checked herself one last time in the mirror, and then went to the front porch to wait for Wade.

The knock on the front door startled Wade. He was smiling as he grabbed the corsage of white lilies and pink roses as he prepared to leave. He opened the door, and the smile died on his face. Arlene stood on his stoop, wet and crying.

Arlene noticed his clothes, then saw the corsage, and putting two and two together, began crying harder. "Oh, Wade!"

"Arlene, what are you doing here?" Wade stood in the doorway, surprised that his cheating ex would show up at his home.

She sniffed, and then crossed her arms protectively around herself. "I didn't know what to do."

She was getting soaked standing outside so Wade backed up and indicated she should come in. "You didn't know what to do about what? What's wrong, Arlene?"

She covered her face with her hands, and then pushed her hair out of her eyes. "I'm in trouble, Wade. Please, you have to help me. Please." Her blue eyes filled with tears. The desperation in them tugged at his heart. Wade knew he still had some residual feelings for her based on their past, but he held back. He was with Melissa now, and whatever was going on with Arlene wasn't his problem. He wouldn't ask again.

"Arlene, whatever it is, you should take it up with your lover. Now, if you'll excuse me, I'm late."

"Where are you going? On a date?"

"Not that it's any of your business, but yes." He reached to open the front door again, intent on ushering her out to her car.

"I'm pregnant."

Wade slammed the door shut.

He turned and looked at her. "What?"

"Six weeks. I'm six weeks pregnant, Wade." Arlene wrung her hands and wandered to the sofa where she sat down, hanging her head.

Wade blinked, and then exhaled. "Why are you telling me this?" He set the corsage down on the hall table and marched into the living room.

"Because, Wade, we were still together then."

"And you were cheating on me!"

Arlene flinched. "I know. But it may still be yours." She kept her eyes cast down.

Wade began to pace. "Why are you here, Arlene? Why aren't you telling this to your lover? Let him deal with it!" Anger seeped into his words. The repercussions of what she was saying began to slowly dawn. If, in fact, the baby turned out to be his, where did that leave him and Melissa? He knew he wouldn't abandon his own child, not even over being angry at its cheating mother. But could he let his own baby be raised by some other man? He knew he couldn't. Dammit. He couldn't just walk away.

"I did tell him." Arlene remained wrapped into a tight ball, hugging herself and rocking back and forth on the edge of the couch.

"And? What did Mr. Wonderful have to say?"

"He said he couldn't help me."

Wade blew a gasket. "That bastard! Who is he, Arlene? Just tell me, and I'll go right now and make him do right by you if he is the father." Seeing the woman he'd once planned his whole life around so miserable and broken, even if by her own choices, ripped at his heart. He wanted to fix this, but didn't know how, or if he should.

Arlene glanced his way. "I can't tell you."

Wade took a deep breath, and then went to sit beside her.

Calmer than he felt, he said, "Look, I know it's not ideal. I get it. It's someone I know. Your resistance to telling me says so, but Arlene, he can't just treat you like you don't matter. It's not right. I don't care if he says he doesn't love you, but if it turns out he's the father, he needs to take responsibility." He waited three seconds and added, "Just as I will if the baby is mine."

Arlene's eyes lit with hope, but as thoughts raced through her head, the light dimmed again. "It's not that he doesn't love me."

Wade reached out and placed a comforting hand on her knee. "Then what is it? What's this guy's problem?"

She hesitated, knowing her next words would shock him. She looked away. "He's married."

The comforting hand was quickly removed, and Wade covered his eyes, massaging his temples. "Arlene!"

"I know! You don't have to say it."

"I think I do. How could you be so gullible? Why would you do that?"

"I don't know. I just don't know." Her voice sounded strangled as tears threatened to overtake her.

A full minute passed in silence. The only sound in the room was Arlene sobbing.

"Okay. One way or the other, it's going to be okay. You just have to tell me, Arlene. I need to know if I'm going to help you, who is he? I won't get mad, I promise." He waited, doing his best to maintain his cool. He'd made a promise, and he was determined to keep it.

Arlene watched Wade, watched him close his eyes and concentrate on breathing. She knew he was mentally preparing himself. She didn't want to tell him, but he wouldn't help her unless he knew, and she couldn't deal with this on her own. She wanted Wade's help. Wanted

Wade to be the father. She wanted Wade back, but not like this, and yet this is what was happening. Wade set the condition, and she would have to take the risk of his anger and tell him.

"It's Bart."

Wade's eyes popped wide open. "My cousin?"

"Yes, but Wade—"

"You cheated on me with Bart? Bart Walker? For the love of God, Arlene, why? What about Mary? Did either of you think about Mary? The kids?" Wade leapt up and began pacing.

"He said he wasn't happy, that they weren't happy anymore—"

"So what? Even if that's true, they're still married! I'm going to kick his ass!" Wade grabbed his keys as his anger trampled all over his promise to Arlene not to get mad. He headed for the front door.

"No, Wade! You can't! She doesn't know!" Arlene ran after him, grabbing his arm and trying to pull him back inside.

Wade turned. "That's the only good thing you've told me. I'm not going to tell her, but I am going to have some words with Bart. He can't just get off Scott-free after cheating on his wife...with *my* girlfriend! No way. He's going to face the consequences, and if he is the father, Arlene, he's going to pay. I'm talking child support for the rest of the kid's life. I don't care if he has to work two jobs and lie to Mary to do it, he's going to do the right thing." Wade yanked his arm free and ran to his truck, jumping in. Arlene stood in the doorway and watched him go, tears in her eyes and a small smile on her lips.

A corsage of white lilies and pink roses sat forgotten on the hall table

Chapter 6

Twenty minutes came and went an hour before. Melissa sent a third text.

Wade, where are you? I'm really worried. Are you okay? Please call me.

Her previous two messages remained unanswered. She stood and looked down the road from beneath the porch overhang. Rain fell in sheets now. Lightning lit the sky, and the fact that Wade hadn't made it to her house yet, nor had he called or answered her texts, had her heart pounding with fear. Thunder rumbled making her jump. She hit number two on her speed dial. It rang twice.

"What is it, Mel?"

"Jed, something's wrong!"

Jed heard the strain in his sister's voice and stopped throwing darts immediately. He looked around at his buddies who were all tossing back a beer at the Wharf Bar & Grill, then walked toward the exit to get away from all the noise. "What's wrong? Is it mom? Is she okay?"

"No, it's Wade. Oh, Jed. He was supposed to be here almost an hour ago, but he hasn't shown up!" She was near crazy with worry.

"Slow down. You realize it's raining cats and dogs outside, right? He's probably just stuck in traffic. Have you called him?" He glanced out the back door and watched the rain filling the potholes in the parking lot.

"I've texted him three times and called once. He hasn't answered. It's not like him, Jed. I think something has happened. Can you try to call? Maybe go by his place and see if he's okay?"

The sob in his sister's voice and her plea got him. Melissa had never asked him for anything, and now she was, and it was a valid request. He couldn't say no. "Alright. I'll drag Joe with me. He needs a break anyway. He's losing his ass at darts. I'll call you once I get there and find out what's going on, okay? Stay by your phone and stay put. I don't need to be worrying about you, too."

"Thank you, thank you, thank you! Be careful. It's really bad out there." She suddenly realized her brother would be putting himself at risk driving over to Wade's in this mess, but she had to know.

"I will. And you call me if he shows up."

"Will do."

Jed hung up. "Damn." He was about to polish off his beer but thought better of it. If he was going to navigate in this storm, he needed his wits about him. He dropped it into the trash can as he went back inside.

"Hey, Joe, stop throwing away your money and come with me. There's a small emergency. Wade might be in trouble."

Joe pushed his hat back on his blond head and threw the dart, hitting the wall. "Yeah, guess you might've just saved my rent, man."

The guys booed them for leaving, but each offered to help if Jed needed it. They left, heading out in Jed's truck. There was a lot of water on the road, and it was better to be safe in a larger vehicle than sorry in Joe's Honda Accord.

"So, where're we going?" Joe buckled his seatbelt and settled back.

"To Wade's place. He was supposed to pick Melissa up over an hour ago now and hasn't shown up. She tried calling and stuff, but no answer."

"That's not like Wade. He's the responsible one."

Jed leaned up and wiped the fog off the windshield with his sleeve, then reached down to turn on the defroster to clear it. "I know. That's why we're going over there. Mel would've jumped into her own truck if I'd said no, and I'm not about to let her put herself in danger. She hasn't even been driving that long, but even if she had, I wouldn't let her do it."

"Yeah, I get it. I wish my sister was as sweet as yours. Nancy is a royal pain in my butt! I'd take Melissa any day you want to swap out." Joe chuckled to himself.

Jed shot him a sideways glance. "Not gonna happen. Nancy's choice of friends would drive me right up the wall."

"That's what I'm sayin'. Those uber-religious freaks get on my nerves. I can't believe Nancy fell for their nonsense. I'm all for Jesus, man, but those dudes are one sandwich short of a picnic, you know what I mean? I'm talkin' dancing with snakes, speakin' in tongues, and hatin' on anyone who isn't just like them. I've tried to talk to her about it, but she's so damn hooked into that boy, Dean, that she's becoming a regular cult case."

Jed turned the corner and took the main road across town. Most of the traffic lights were blinking bright yellow and not working properly. "You and your parents might need to stage an intervention if you can't expose that whacko Dean for what he really is. He's just manipulating her."

Jed screeched to a halt. Joe flew forward in his seatbelt, but was stopped short of hitting the dash. "What the hell, man?"

"Sorry, Joe. You okay?" Jed patted his buddy's shoulder, then pointed. "There's a large branch in the street. I almost didn't see it."

Joe looked, squinting through the water sloshing onto the windshield despite the wipers swiping at the deluge. "Oh, dude! That woulda messed up your truck." He gave Jed a thumbs up. "Good catch."

Jed maneuvered around it and proceeded with caution. The winds were picking up, and leaves and smaller branches were flying everywhere. "Well, at least we're halfway there. I haven't seen any cars stalled on the side of the road, have you?"

"Naw. Nothing."

It took another twenty minutes to get there. Usually, it would only have been five to ten minutes, but the heavy rain and increasing wind velocity slowed their commute. Jed pulled into Wade's driveway. His home was a converted, detached garage like his own, but unlike Jed, Wade rented his from the people next door. The Walker family lived just down the street from their old high school, and Wade moved out over a year ago. He worked to pay for his privacy, but the rent wasn't near as much as it would be had he not known the Smiths from whom he rented. Five hundred a month for seven hundred square feet of bachelor pad with utilities paid was a good deal. The Smiths liked Wade. They knew he wouldn't trash their rental, and he maintained their yard for them as a bonus.

"I don't see his car, but isn't that Arlene's?" Joe pointed toward the red Camry.

Jed nodded. He knew Arlene's car well. Seeing it at Wade's when Wade was supposed to be dating his sister, supposed to be *on* a date with his sister, made his blood begin to boil. If he found out Wade was cheating on Melissa with his sworn ex-girlfriend, he was going to kill him.

Arlene saw headlights through the window blinds. She hadn't expected Wade to be back so soon. She hoped it was because he changed his mind about confronting Bart. She ran to the front door and opened it just as Jed Ryan was about to knock.

"Jesus, you scared me!" She jumped back a step, her hand covering her heart.

"Arlene, where's Wade?" Jed pushed past her and looked inside.

"He's not here. What's wrong?" She looked out at his truck and saw Joe sitting in the passenger seat.

"Where'd he go?" Jed turned and faced her.

Arlene hesitated, not wanting to share her business with anyone.

"Arlene, where is Wade?" Jed asked again, slowing down his words, emphasizing his loss of patience.

"He went to Bart's." She offered a half-truth.

Jed stared a hole through her head. "Finally found out, did he?"

"Found out what?" She placed her hands on her hips and faced him, eyeing him with suspicion.

"That you and Bart have been screwing around," he said, matter of fact.

Arlene's eyes popped wide. "How did you—?"

"Everyone knew, Arlene. Everyone except Wade. You two weren't very discreet."

A car horn sounded indicating Joe was ready to go. Jed walked to the door and waved at him to hold on a moment longer.

"Why are you here looking for him anyway?" Arlene's words snapped. She didn't like anyone else knowing what she'd done.

"Because he was supposed to be on a date with my sister over an hour ago, that's why. What the hell are you doing here?" Jed let his anger fly.

"He's dating your sister? The crippled one?" Arlene's words left her mouth unfiltered.

Jed stepped closer and jabbed a finger in her face.

"Don't you call her that! You watch your mouth, Arlene Richards." The look in his eyes warned her not to say anything denigrating again.

"I'm sorry. I didn't mean it like that. I'm just surprised, that's all. He never said."

"You didn't answer my question," Jed persisted.

Arlene, cornered and threatened by both Jed, and the news about Wade dating his sister, tossed out her next words with deliberation. "I'm pregnant. That's why I'm here. That's why Wade is at Bart's. He's warning him to stay away from me."

Jed took that news like a punch to the gut. It wasn't that he cared himself, but this was going to devastate Melissa. "The baby is Wade's?" His eyebrow rose in question.

Taking a deep breath, Arlene let the poisonous lie fall from her lips.

"Yes. It's his and we're getting back together. You know Wade. You know he'd never walk away from his own child, his responsibility."

Jed stepped back. He did know Wade, and he knew if he was just confronted with this kind of news, he'd do right by Arlene no matter how wrong the girl was. He also knew that this left his baby sister out in the cold. His mom was right. Wade was going to break Melissa's heart. He turned and headed back to his truck.

Arlene followed him out. "Where are you going now?"

"To Bart's!" He didn't even bother to turn around and look at her. He couldn't. Just the sight of her sickened him because he knew Arlene Richards and her cheating, scheming ways were about to destroy his sister. He needed to pound someone and since he'd never hit a girl, he was going to keep his promise and knock the hell out of Wade.

Arlene watched as yet another person sped off to Bart's house. She turned to go back inside and wait. It was then she spotted the corsage Wade had been holding when she arrived earlier. She opened the box and lifted out the dainty wrist bouquet of white lilies and pink roses. She tried it on, sniffed the sweet fragrance, and then tossed it out into the rain.

"Sorry, Melissa. He's mine."

"Bart, we need to talk." Wade stood on his cousin's front doorstep, rigid with rage. He peeked around and caught Mary looking at him from the living room. He gave her a wave, and then grabbed Bart's arm and yanked him outside.

Bart looked at his cousin, saw the fury radiating off him in waves. He knew the moment had come. He reached back and closed the door leaving his wife inside.

"What is it, Wade?"

Bart stared at his younger cousin. For as long as he could remember, Wade was the 'golden' child of the family. He was popular in high school, played football, baseball, and made good grades. He never stepped out of line and did everything right. He was exactly the opposite of Bart who hung out with the wrong crowd, skipped classes, and although he played summer sports as a kid, avoided it in high school because his friends said only dorks did that sort of thing. That attitude carried over into adult life even though he had a great wife, and two healthy, happy children. He still made self-destructive decisions. Wade had everything, including beautiful, sexy Arlene. Taking her away from him had felt good. He wasn't sorry.

Wade swung and punched Bart in the mouth. The crack of knuckles splitting a lip was a satisfying sound to his ears. Bart reeled backwards and covered his face.

"Son of a—"

"Shut up and listen, Bart!" Wade grabbed a handful of Bart's hair and clenched his fist in warning. "Arlene came by tonight. She told me she's pregnant."

"So what?" came the muffled reply.

Wade yanked Bart's hair pulling his face up to look at him. "It's possible that your sorry butt is the father. Yeah, I know about the two of you. I don't want to hear any excuses from you either. When the baby is born, you're taking a paternity test. If it's yours, you're going to do right by Arlene and pay child support."

"And what if I refuse? You can't make me do anything, Wade! I'm older than you, remember?"

"Oh, really? That's how you want to play this?" Wade let go of Bart and reached for the doorknob.

"What're you doing?" Bart grabbed his hand and jumped in front of the door.

Wade glared at him. "Either you do right by Arlene, or I tell Mary what you've done."

"You can't do that." Bart spoke in a hushed tone. "She'd leave me and take my kids."

"And you'd deserve it! But Mary doesn't deserve to be hurt by your asinine actions. So, this is the deal, Bart. You will do the right thing. If you do the right thing, she'll never know. I won't tell her. But if you don't submit to the paternity test, I'm telling her, and I won't care what happens after that. You're doing this. Who knows? You might get lucky and not actually be the father. Arlene doesn't want you anyway." He turned to leave.

"What do you mean by that? Arlene loves me!" Bart stomped after his cousin.

Wade looked over his shoulder. "No, Bart, she doesn't. She just used you because she was afraid of losing me."

"Yeah? Well, what are you going to do if you're the father? You gonna take her back? Good luck with having my sloppy seconds, Wade!" Bart shot off his mouth.

Wade hit him again.

"Dammit!" Bart clutched his nose.

Wade stood over his cousin who was bent over spitting out blood onto the grass. "She was mine first. The only person who had sloppy seconds was you, Bart."

He turned and marched to his truck. Before he slid into the driver's seat, he added, "And stop wearing that crappy cologne. You stink like a damn pimp!" Wade got in, slammed the door, and drove away.

Jed pulled into Bart's driveway. The guy was sitting outside nursing a fat lip. He got out and approached Wade's cousin.

"I'm looking for Wade. Has he been here?"

The rain, which had slowed, began to come down in earnest once again. Bart moved under the overhang of his porch. "He's been and gone. Why?"

"Because he was supposed to be somewhere tonight, and he didn't show up. We've all been worried. What happened to your face?" Jed eyed the swelling around Bart's mouth and nose.

"Wade happened. He sucker-punched me."

"Because of Arlene?"

Bart shook his head. "Christ, does everyone know?"

"Almost. I'm sure your wife will be the last. Where did Wade go?"

"How the hell would I know? He didn't share that info with me. Probably back to his hussy of a girlfriend."

Jed swung and punched Bart on the jaw.

"Damn, son of a... What was that for?"

Jed stared daggers at Bart. "Don't you ever call my sister a hussy. You do so again, and I'll kill you!"

Bart looked confused. "Your sister? Arlene isn't your sister. What the heck are you talking about?"

Jed's eyes opened wide. "You said Wade was going back to his girlfriend."

Bart glared at him. "Yeah. Arlene. Who did you think I meant?"

"Wade is dating my sister, Melissa. That's who I thought you meant."

Bart looked surprised, then he laughed. "Well, isn't that special? So, ole Wade was cheating on Arlene with your sister."

Offended, Jed let loose. "Wade broke up with Arlene a month ago. He's been dating my sister since. The only person cheating around here is you!"

"Well, if he hasn't cheated, he's about to because he sure did come here to defend Arlene's honor, not that she has any."

"I don't give a damn about her or you. I only care about my sister and finding Wade. You sure you don't know where he went?"

"Like I said, probably back home. He said Arlene came by earlier. She's probably still there." Bart leaned back against the house.

Jed glared at Bart showing his anger with every second that passed. He knew Arlene was at Wade's, and now he knew he would be heading back there. He sighed and turned to leave.

"Good luck with explaining your face to your wife," Jed sneered.

"Screw you, Jed." Bart's comment was weak. He knew he would have some explaining to do, just as Jed knew he would lie about the bruises on his face when he went back inside.

Jed got in his truck. Joe looked at him with one eyebrow raised. "Good shot, man." He gave Jed a fist bump.

Jed returned the gesture half-hearted. He pulled out his cell phone and stared at it.

"What's wrong, Jed?" Joe saw the anguish on his friend's face.

"I don't know how I'm going to tell Mel."

"Tell her what?"

He looked at Joe. "That Wade is going back to Arlene."

Joe blew out a breath and ran a hand over his face. "Well, you've never lied to her. Don't start now. The sooner she knows, the sooner she can grieve, and then get over it. She's a good girl, your sister. Hell, I'd date her if that would help."

Jed chuckled with derision. "No way, Joe. I can't handle any of my friends trying to date my sister again. At this rate, I'd be punching the lot of you."

"Well, I don't want to end up like Bart. I wonder what he's going to tell his wife."

"He'll lie. He's a sorry sack of dirt."

Jed dialed his sister's number and waited for her to pick up. Dread filled him, and he knew before he could go home and help her through this, he had to make one last stop. Wade deserved the pounding he was about to receive, but he sort-of regretted having to administer it. They'd been friends for a while, and now, it was over.

Melissa stared at her phone. She couldn't believe what she'd just heard. Tears filled her eyes, blinding her. She couldn't see anything, and she didn't want to. He stood her up. He stood her up for his ex-girlfriend who was pregnant. She knew she didn't stand a chance against Arlene on a normal day, and now there was a baby between them. If anyone else had told her all of this, she would've denied it. Wade wouldn't just put her aside for Arlene, not like this, but coming from her own brother, who would never lie to her, and coupled with the fact that Wade was not returning her calls drove the truth home. Sobs wracked her body. She felt as if her heart had been ripped from her chest.

She'd opened herself up and trusted him, and he'd promised not to hurt her. He'd promised, and then he broke that promise along with her heart. The pain in her soul felt worse than any physical pain she'd ever experienced. Without thought, she stood and grabbed her crutches. Before she knew it, she was sitting inside her old truck, soaked to the skin, and shaking. She started the engine and drove out of the driveway. She didn't know where she was going and could hardly see through the rain and her tears. All she knew was she needed to get away. She couldn't face her mom, who sat inside her bedroom watching television, unaware of all that had occurred. She wouldn't be able to face Jed once he got home. She needed to be alone.

Each mile she drove was another mile away from Wade, and away from anyone looking at her with pity. She already knew she wasn't good enough for Wade. She didn't need anyone's sympathy. What she'd feared all along had come true. Somehow, she'd just been a fling for him, a curiosity he needed to satisfy. It was never her he loved, but Arlene all along. He said he'd wait a lifetime for her, but he lied.

Why? Why, Wade?

She could barely breathe. Each breath was a chore. Her chest hurt, and she felt sick. She realized she was close to Pelican's Cove and turned off onto the long road down to the beach. As she drove, she remembered every look, every touch, and every single kiss they shared. *Did he mean any of it or was it all just fun and games? Tease the disabled girl. She's an easy target!*

The road was dark. There were no lights along this stretch, and the moon was covered by storm clouds unloading their wrath upon the earth. As she made her way down the hill, she missed the turn for the beach. Suddenly, her truck began to slide down the slippery boat ramp. She slammed the brake, but it was too late. Her truck plunged into the water. Then it began to sink.

Panicked, Melissa tried to unlatch her seatbelt but couldn't find the release button. Water filled the cab of the truck as she struggled.

"Help!" she screamed. "Help me, oh, God!"

She yanked at the belt trying once again to find the release. It finally gave and she was suspended, floating inside the vehicle. The water was up to her neck. She pulled the door handle, but the pressure of the waves against the door was too great. As her head went under, she fumbled for the button to unroll the window, but the engine was flooded and no longer running. The electronics weren't working. She smacked at the glass, then grabbed one of her crutches and tried to break it with the metal pole. She couldn't gather enough momentum in the rushing water. In seconds, her air ran out, and as she began losing consciousness, thoughts flashed through her mind. *Mom! Jed! I love you. Wade...Wade... I love you.*

Chapter 7

November, 2055

Wade stared down at the picture in the tarnished silver frame. It usually sat by his bed, right next to his medications and the picture of his daughter, Charlie—Charlene Denise Walker Talbot to be exact, along with her husband Dave, and their son, his grandson, Rory Wade Talbot. He stared at the lovely face smiling inside the frame, she with the sable hair, soft brown eyes, and dolphin spray creating rainbows around her head. It was one of the best days of his life. She would always be young and beautiful no matter how old he got. And he was old now.

His hair, once blond, was now gray, and his green eyes had clouded over with the beginnings of cataracts, becoming blurred. He needed glasses to see anything anymore, and the wire frames perched on his nose held thick lenses. He touched the image and smiled to himself. Wade glanced up at the calendar on the wall. November 16th. The date was circled in a red heart. He set the picture back down on the nightstand, arranging it just so. He kissed his fingertips and touched her face. As he leaned forward to stand, he felt the wind leave his lungs. Getting up was getting harder and often knocked the air out of him. His knees hurt from rheumatism, and his back hurt just because. He made it to his feet and grabbed his cane. After slipping into his jacket and donning his hat, he picked up his keys and a single long-stem pink rose. Slowly, he shuffled out to the waiting cab. He couldn't drive anymore, not with his eyesight and declining health.

"Where to?" the cabbie asked.

"Woodlawn." Wade sat back and tried to enjoy the ride. It was a cold day with a nip in the wind. The weatherman predicted rain in the coming days, and clouds already began to gather. He didn't like the rain. It brought back too many bad memories. It had rained that night, the awful night that changed everything so long ago.

He'd lost everything that night. First, his friend, Jed, who'd come to his home, and socked him in the jaw, and rightly so, but for the wrong reasons. And then...Melissa.

Wade teared up. He still couldn't think about that moment when Jed called him the next day to tell him the coast guard and police found her...still inside the cab of her truck...without experiencing sharp pain in his chest. There was no question as to what sent her out into the storm that night, but what was unclear was whether or not it was an accident, or if she meant to harm herself. Wade just couldn't believe she would commit suicide, not over him or for any reason. She'd gone through so much in her short life. She was a fighter, but the police investigation was inconclusive, even if the autopsy wasn't. Melissa had drowned.

Jed had never forgiven him or even himself for being the one to deliver the news of Arlene and Wade's baby. It was especially hard on him because it turned out that the baby was Bart's, not Wade's. Arlene's lies were revealed, and Wade never spoke to her again.

He left Pelican's Bay that fall, as planned, and after earning his law degree, stayed in Boston for over twenty years. He met a nice girl named Anna, and they married. Charlie was their daughter. Still, he never got over Melissa, and eventually, their marriage fell apart. They divorced when Charlie was six, and he never remarried. Once his daughter graduated high school, he moved back to his hometown. He'd been there ever since practicing law, working on the environmental issues in his state, and dedicating his every success to his one true love.

He saw Arlene about a year after he moved back. She was sitting on the patio of the local Mexican restaurant, El Tortillaria, sipping a large fountain drink and eating tacos. He barely recognized her. She'd nearly doubled in size since he last saw her. Next to her was a girl that looked almost exactly like her. He assumed she was Arlene's daughter. But the giveaway was the man sitting across from them both; his cousin, Bart. Wade had heard through his mother that Bart's marriage fell apart not long after he'd gone off to Boston. Mary found out about Arlene when she came to their home and baldly announced that she was pregnant with Bart's child. She wasn't even sure about it at that point. The DNA test came after she gave birth, but she was denied Wade, so she stole Bart. The breakup of his marriage drove him to drink, and Mary wouldn't let him see his kids because of it. Wade had noticed the Cerveza in front of him while he stuffed a burrito in his mouth. He'd decided immediately to eat somewhere else that day. The last thing he'd wanted then was to come face to face with those two.

The taxi driver made a right turn and pulled into the long drive through Woodlawn.

"Which way?" he asked.

"The top of the hill. Over there by the statue of Gabriel." Wade pointed, squinting through his glasses toward the tall sculpture under the two giant palm trees.

The gray and yellow cab climbed the road and pulled off onto the shoulder. "This okay?" The cab driver, whose name on his license said it was Antonio, turned to ask.

Wade looked out across the manicured lawn. "Yes, this is fine." He opened the door and started to get out, then stopped. "You'll wait?"

Antonio nodded. "Si, si. Take your time."

Wade nodded. Of course he'd say that. The meter was still running, but he didn't care. This would be the last time he visited this place. He stepped off the shoulder onto the green grass and slowly made his way toward the statue. It took thirty-three steps in all, but when he stopped, he looked down and read the name on the marker at the feet of the angel, Gabriel.

Melissa Katherine Ryan

Born November 16, 1986

Died June 4, 2005

Beloved daughter, sister, and friend

Next to her marker was Jed, *Jedidiah Michael Ryan*, and their mom, *Katherine Eleanor Taft Ryan*. Jed's wife, Sue, was still living, so her marker lay blank next to Jed's. On the other side of the statue was another blank marker, a place holder. It had cost nearly all the money Wade had saved to purchase it, but he wanted to be near Melissa when his time came. It was all he'd ever wanted.

"Happy birthday, sweetheart." He reached into his jacket and pulled out the single long-stem pink rose and laid it gently on her grave. Wade leaned onto his cane and let out a heavy sigh. "I know you're probably tired of hearing me say it, but I'm so sorry. I never wanted to hurt you, Melissa. Never. You meant the world to me. Once I found you, I didn't want to let go, not for anything or anyone. There was never any chance for Arlene after you. Baby or not, I wouldn't have gone back to her, but I did hope then that if the baby was mine, you'd understand my need to make sure it knew me, knew that I cared. I would've done right by the child. I'm sure you would have understood if I had the chance to explain it, but that chance never came. We never even had our third date. I never got to tell you..." Wade wiped a tear from his eye. He reached into his back pocket for a handkerchief and blew his nose.

"All I wanted that night was to be able to tell you how much I loved you. I still love you. I was going to marry you, Melissa Ryan." A half-laugh, half-sob escaped him. His voice dropped to a whisper. "You were my girl, my only true love. I will always love you, in this lifetime, and the next. God willing, I'm going to find you again. I promise." His voice cracked. "I'll find you and make things right, give you everything you deserve and then some. You'll be surrounded by so much love you won't know what to do with it all. And I won't screw it up. I promise." He stopped and rubbed at the pain in his chest.

"God," he whispered, his cloudy eyes glancing up, "just give me one more chance. Give *us* one more chance. Please!"

Wade closed his eyes as the familiar sorrow washed over him. He prayed that God would reunite them somehow. He'd been so lonely. Fifty years later and he still talked to her every day. No other woman had been able to fill the hole in his heart. The closest one that came to doing so was his daughter, Charlie. He poured all the love he had inside of him into her and his grandson, and still there was more, but no outlet for it all. So, he began coming to Woodlawn one day a week since returning home to Florida thirty years ago. Each time, he brought a pink rose and laid it on the resting place of his beloved.

A cool wind buffeted the palms. The subtle sound soothed him. After a time, he got himself together and turned to leave. Wade paused, glancing back.

"Sophocles was right, you know. About fate. I have to believe it. I do believe it. Nothing can stop it. Nothing can stop me from finding you again. I'll be seeing you again, my love…soon."

He blew her a kiss and began the journey of thirty-three steps back to the taxi. He looked around the manicured grounds as they drove back down the hill and out the front gate of the cemetery for the last time.

That night, Wade climbed into bed, more tired than he'd ever been in his life. He picked up the aged silver framed photograph of Melissa laughing at the bottlenose dolphin. The color had faded to a warm sepia over the last fifty years, but he could still see her clearly in his memory. He could still hear her laughter, and he could still taste the sweetness of her lips. He kissed her picture, and took off his glasses, setting them on the nightstand. After turning out the light, he settled into his pillow and clutched the silver-framed keepsake close to his heart. A smile teased his lips as his thoughts drifted back to the day they played tourists, on a boat ride off the coast of Florida.

The sun rose the next day, as expected, but Wade Walker did not. His spirit was now free to find the only woman he'd ever loved.

Chapter 8

Fall Semester, 2073

Portland, Oregon

Elizabeth Eaton was late again. She finally found a parking space on campus and jumped out of her vintage-style VW SmartBug. The bright yellow color stood out in a sea of silver and black smart cars. She plugged hers into the parking terminal and ran inside the four-story building heading to class. It was her third day of Impressionistic Painting, and she looked forward to it because today was the day they would begin working on painting a live model. It was to be their semester project.

She took the stairs two at a time and got into her classroom just as the instructor began assigning workstations.

"Nice of you to join us, Elizabeth." Mr. Jeffries gave her a sardonic look, but the smile tugging at his mustache told her he was probably used to college students wandering in late. "Take that one over there."

He pointed to the far side of the room. The open easel was set up with the sun at her back. It was a good spot. The model would be standing in good light.

"These easels will be yours throughout the rest of the semester." Mr. Jeffries walked the inner circle of all the stations addressing the students. "You're responsible for keeping them clean. That means your brushes, your palettes, and the paints supplied to you. Remember that this stuff is costly. Your tuition paid for it and if anything happens to your supplies, you're responsible for replacing them. Got it?"

"Got it," everyone replied in unison.

The females in the class were calm, but the males were excited. Elizabeth heard two of them whispering to each other.

"Bring on the naked lady, already!" said the boy next to her with dyed blue hair. His partner, a tall young man with mocha-colored skin and hazel eyes, laughed.

"Shoot, Brett, you wouldn't even know what to do with one."

"Pipe down." Mr. Jeffries admonished the two. "Now, when the model comes in, there is to be no talking. You do not engage the model. You will not make faces, sounds, or try to give instructions to the model. You simply begin painting. I've already instructed our model on the necessary pose, and that is the pose that will be maintained until this portrait is complete. I expect to see identifiable elements of impressionism, people. Your grade will depend on it. Extra credit to those who manage to move me with your interpretations of the lighting. And no snickering or snide comments. Take this seriously.

You're all adults now." The instructor looked around at everyone, nodded, and then went to the door.

Elizabeth squeezed some basic neutral shades of paint onto her palette. She chose a brush, made sure her thinner was poured into the glass jar, and laid newspaper out under it all. Satisfied she was ready, she looked up only to hear the two classmates next to her groan in disappointment.

A young man walked in behind Mr. Jeffries wearing a white robe. Elizabeth didn't see him clearly until he came out from behind the instructor and walked to the dais in the center of the room. He faced the windows and Elizabeth.

Her breath caught in her throat.

The sound captured his attention, and he looked at her. Their eyes met, his as green as spring leaves, and hers as dark as warm cinnamon. Her heartbeat sped up and she swallowed hard. A blush ran up her neck, and he smiled slowly as he untied the belt and slipped the robe off his broad shoulders. It fell to his feet, and he stood naked before her.

The student next to her called Brett noticed the eye contact between his classmate and the model and reached over to slap his friend on the arm, pointing at the two of them.

"Damn. You two know each other or something?" Brett chuckled, and his friend snorted.

"No talking!" Mr. Jeffries' voice rose above theirs.

Elizabeth looked down at her blank canvas, her cheeks hot, but all she saw were sexy green eyes, dirty blond hair with a slight curl, and broad shoulders that tapered to a narrow waist, and further down to muscular thighs, and shapely calves. She didn't even want to think about what she'd skipped over, but the impression was there.

Well, Mr. Jeffries said capture the impression so...be brave. You can do it!" Her inner cheerleader tried giving her the pep talk, and she rallied as best as she could manage. Lifting her eyes, she peered around her canvas.

He was still watching her.

She tried to ignore his direct stare, and began working from one point; his eyes. Her hand expertly created every nuance of those eyes and the surrounding face. She drew the shapes and lines as if she'd drawn him a million times before. The morning sun slanted in, filtering through the windows, and surrounded him in a surreal glow of white light. Elizabeth tried to capture the feeling it incited within her, but how did one capture déjà vu on canvas?

The hour passed, and before she knew it, class was over. The model bent down and picked up his robe. Covered once again, he headed out of the room. Some of the students were already packing up their things. Elizabeth rinsed her brushes and laid them on the newspaper, then she spread a sheet over her canvas and placed more newspaper over her paints. She glanced at the now empty dais, strangely saddened he was no longer there. With a sigh, she picked up her purse and book bag and headed out with her fellow stragglers.

"See you all on Friday," Mr. Jeffries said, waving at Elizabeth before locking up the classroom.

She nodded and looked up and down the hall wondering where the young man with the green eyes had gone.

Matt McCandless sat in his car checking messages on his iWatch. The hologram spun through the list hovering above his wrist. He opened a few with a touch of his finger and deleted the rest. Finished, he touched his thumb to the ignition and started his car. As he looked up, he saw the girl from art class dash across the parking lot to a bright yellow SmartBug. She unplugged the charger, and pushed the button for the cord to reel back in.

He smiled. She was definitely the 'artsy' type, and her choice of vehicle fit right in with that image. He remembered the moment their eyes met. He couldn't look away, and the longer he stared, the deeper she blushed. For some reason, he'd felt absurdly happy about it, so much so that standing in that room stark naked hadn't bothered him at all. It was his first modeling gig, a means by which to earn a little extra cash after his ecology class.

He hadn't been sure how he was going to feel about standing naked in front of strangers, but when he saw she was more embarrassed about it than he was, it suddenly didn't seem so bad. Still, it was all he could do to maintain control of himself. He felt a small measure of pride in having flooded his own brain with thoughts guaranteed to prevent a humiliating incident. It wasn't easy, either, but now that he was dressed, and sitting in his own vehicle, he let his thoughts fly.

She opened the door and dropped her bag inside. It was pink, just like her sneakers, and the T-shirt she was wearing. The color suited her and complemented her long, dark hair. He waited until she gracefully slipped into her car and drove out of the parking lot before backing out. Now, he couldn't wait until Friday to see her again.

Chapter 9

Elizabeth looked around the unfamiliar room, then at the canvas before her. She was painting a seascape. Large rocks jutted out of the water creating a private bay. Between brush strokes, she kept falling over into the sand and having to begin again. Each time, the view changed from daylight to darkness, from clear skies to thunderclouds. A large wave loomed in the distance as thunder cracked. She painted as fast as she could, trying to beat the rain. The sound was so loud, it knocked her down again, and this time, she was pulled into the water as the wave crashed up onto the beach and over the easel. It dragged her down deep into the ocean where she couldn't breathe. She beat her fists on the glass holding her inside the cab of a truck. It wouldn't break no matter how hard she hit it. The loud 'whoosh' of currents whipping her around clashed with the thunder overhead. One loud crack broke the glass as she struggled for air.

Her eyes flew open, and she sat up in bed terrified and drenched in sweat.

Outside, the rain fell hard, slapping against her bedroom window as lightning streaked the sky. Elizabeth threw her covers off and sat on the side of the bed with her feet planted firmly on the floor. Her heart raced, and she felt as if she'd run a marathon.

She'd had these dreams as a child, and never understood where they came from. She'd never once in her life had a close call with drowning. Heck, she avoided going into anything deeper than the kiddie pool, so it was a mystery why she'd been haunted by such nightmares. After the age of ten, they trickled off, and she hadn't experienced one in years, until tonight. She had no idea what triggered the old nightmares but figured it must be the storm raging outside. She got up and went to the window, looking out.

Her tiny apartment overlooked a hillside that traveled down to a bridge that spanned the creek. It was usually a calming sight, but tonight, the creek appeared flooded. If it rose any higher, it would block the bridge for most of the day unless the rain stopped soon.

As Elizabeth sat watching the storm from her window, the winds died down, and the thunder grew distant. Calm again, she went back to bed and lay there wondering for the millionth time why she had nightmares about painting a cove and drowning. Not wanting to fall back asleep thinking about something so scary, she let her mind drift, and a pair of green eyes with a sexy smile filled her thoughts. She sighed. The model from class was very handsome. He was also the first fully naked man she'd ever seen.

Elizabeth recalled his form; strong, tanned, and quite something to behold. Then she remembered other parts of his remarkable body. That thought caused heat to creep up her neck and down her spine. It was such a strange looking appendage, and she hoped to do it justice when painting it. It was rather large to her way of thinking, especially knowing the mechanics of sexual intercourse. She tried to imagine it, but embarrassment washed over her even in the darkness of her own bedroom. She shook off the thought, and adjusted her pillow, determined to go back to sleep. This time, her dreams were pleasant, even a bit heady. Instead of drowning in the ocean, she was basking in the warm regard of a certain, handsome young man who was teasing her with his words, then kissing her silly.

Her first real kiss...

The next morning, she arose at her usual time of seven and got ready for work. Elizabeth loved her part time job. She taught art to disabled kids at the local children's hospital, St. Francis. It was a pilot program in which she only worked ten hours a week, two hours a day, Monday through Friday, but it was beyond rewarding. As it turned out, working on art projects like clay sculpting, watercolor painting, sketching, and pottery design was excellent therapy for the kids hospitalized for all types of disabilities. She decided disabled was not the best description. Handicapped was better because from what she'd learned by teaching them, it wasn't that they couldn't do anything, but rather, had to find a different way to tackle everyday tasks. That would be a handicap, just like in the game of golf—a degree of difficulty whereby a person had to plan out a workable strategy.

She witnessed these remarkable children assessing the assignments, and then finding the best way to accomplish them using the means they had. Then, they executed their plans with courage, devotion, and sheer joy. It made her emotional every time, and it was no small feat that she managed to hold in all her feelings behind smiles that never seemed to end. She loved these kids, and they loved her.

Just the other day, a little boy named Thad, who was born without fully formed arms, showed her how he paints beautiful landscapes by holding his paintbrush with his teeth. His latest creation of dandelions in the wind was so spectacular that Elizabeth found a local art gallery willing to exhibit it along with a few other pieces created by these talented children. All the kids agreed that if any of their pieces sold, they would donate the money to the hospital to help others. It was just this type of generosity of heart that made her job not a job at all, but rather, a tremendous source of happiness and accomplishment.

She threw on a gray and pink striped T-shirt with blue jeans and her pink sneakers. Pink was her favorite color for as long as she could remember, and she wore it a lot. Her hair hung forward onto her face as she tied her shoelaces. Then, she twisted the wayward tresses up and secured them with a pink butterfly clip. A smidge of mascara and lip gloss, and she was ready for her day. She hoisted her backpack off the floor and slung it over her shoulder. She had classes later, History and Government, and she figured she would have just enough time to study for the history chapter test following work.

The sun was shining as she descended the stairs from her second-floor apartment. No more rain in the forecast, but she could smell the damp earth, and everything was bright and green. It was going to be a beautiful day.

Matt tossed his supplies into the stern of his best girl. They'd been in a relationship since he turned sixteen. That was the day his dad took him out back and unveiled the small white boat. She was perfect in every way. She was always ready to go out onto the water, she never fussed at him when he had to work, and she was always waiting for him when he came home. Matt remembered wanting to take her out onto the waves that very day, but his dad stopped him.

"You have to name it first, son. It's bad luck to take a boat out without first naming it and having a proper christening."

Matt had thought about it all night. His boat was beautiful, pure white, and the new love of his life. That next morning, he got up and went straight to the woodshed where he found a can of red paint and a brush. When his dad came out later to see what he was up to, Matt had already finished painting on the name he chose in painstakingly elegant cursive.

Melissa.

"Melissa?" His dad raised an eyebrow in question. "So, who's Melissa? New girlfriend?"

Matt grinned. "Yeah, she's my girl."

His dad had laughed. "When do I get to meet her?"

Matt slapped his dad on the back and winked. "You already did, dad. You gave her to me for my birthday."

"So, there's not really a Melissa?" His dad asked, confused.

Matt dropped the paintbrush into a jar of thinner and whooshed it around. His thoughts turned inward. "I suppose there is a Melissa out there somewhere. I dunno. I just always liked that name. It's pretty, don't ya think?"

Tom McCandless shrugged. "As pretty as any, I guess. All that matters is that you like it because you two will be together for a long time." He reached out and mussed Matt's hair. "Treat her right, son, and she'll always bring you home."

"I will, dad. Can I take you and my girl out later, you know, once the paint dries?"

"I thought you'd never ask!"

Matt and his dad spent that afternoon on the water, fishing. It was one of the best days of his life. It was the day he fell in love with the freedom and independence that came with having his own boat. He loved her. He'd taken to referring to his boat as 'her' and his 'girl' ever since.

That was just six years and thousands of fishing trips ago, and Melissa was still his best girl. The only difference was that now, her bright red letters had faded to a soft pink, and she was showing signs of age. Soon, she'd need a maintenance overhaul and a fresh coat of paint. Also, she resided at his parents' home in Tillamook while he stayed in Portland at a dormitory to attend college. They didn't get to spend as much time together anymore and wouldn't be able to take daily jaunts out into the Pacific until summer. But in the meantime, they were about to spend the day together.

Matt wanted to check on a group of dolphins that showed up the weekend before. One of them appeared pregnant, and about to give birth. He hoped to find a new baby striped dolphin among them.

The waves were still choppy from the rough weather the night before, but nothing his girl couldn't handle. Matt pushed the boat out, and then jumped inside. He slid onto the bench seat and grabbed the oars. Each pull on the oak handles forced the boat further out past the breakers and into calmer water. Once he was well past the shallows, he stowed the oars and started the outboard motor. He kept to the coastline and worked his way south to the tip of the inlet that jutted out from Tillamook Bay. Matt dropped his anchor and watched it sink into the sandbar of the crystal-clear water. As soon as it landed, he opened the cooler he'd placed in the stern and pulled out his lunch and a large zip-lock bag of fresh chopped squid, a favorite treat of striped dolphins.

He ate his own ham and cheese hoagie, a bag of potato chips, and drank from a large canteen of water. The day was peaceful, a bit on the warm side, and quiet. There weren't any tourists on the coastal beach, but he did see an older couple walking arm in arm. Clapping his hands together to knock off any crumbs, he reached for the zip-lock bag. He planned to toss out just a couple of the chunks. He knew that dolphins had a keen sense of both hearing and smell, and he hoped they would pick up on their favorite delicacy as they tasted the water.

An hour passed with no dolphins sighted. He eyed the waves in all directions, disappointed when he found nothing. Matt sighed and reached for the rope to pull anchor when a chirping sound off the starboard bow caught his attention. A rubbery, bluish-gray nose peeked over the side of the boat, and quickly disappeared. He let go of the rope and leaned forward peering into the water.

Suddenly, a shower of sea water doused his back. He turned and saw a fin move about thirty yards out. It stopped, and up popped a striped dolphin, looking for all the world like it was laughing at him.

Matt chuckled.

"Well, hello to you too!" He reached for the bag of squid chunks and tossed a few out toward the mischief maker. "Here ya go, girl. I hope you're a girl, anyway. I wouldn't want to offend you."

The dolphin dove after the floating treats, quickly gobbling them up. She moved in closer, lifting her head above water, and emitted a happy sound.

"More? You must be hungry." He threw a few pieces into the water about two feet from the boat. The dolphin swam closer, inspecting the area and keeping an eye on him, he was sure. She ate the squid, and then, as if deciding this human was okay, came right up to the side of the boat and chirped.

Matt reached over cautiously letting her see that he meant no harm and slowly extended his fingers until the gorgeous mammal pushed her nose into his hand. "So, the guy with squid is acceptable, huh?"

He gently rubbed her nose, and she bobbed her head as if to say, 'yes'. Suddenly, she dove under and swam away. Matt watched in surprise.

"Hey, where are you going? We just made friends!"

The fin disappeared beneath the waves.

Sad to see her go, he once again reached for the rope to pull up anchor. He'd just begun to drag it out of the sandbar when he was splashed from three sides.

"What the—!" He shook off the water and looked out, finding three fully grown dolphins, and one newborn baby.

"So, you were pregnant! And you brought the family to meet me. Well, then, this is cause for a celebration, isn't it?"

Matt grabbed the zip-lock bag and emptied the entire contents of squid chunks over the side. The three adult dolphins snatched up a few, but they seemed to be encouraging the baby to come and partake of the feast. One dolphin pushed two chunks toward the little one with its nose.

"You must be mom," he said. He looked at the baby. "May as well listen to her, little man. She's just doing what moms do, making sure you eat. Try it. Squid is good stuff."

The little dolphin inched forward and tasted the first chunk. Matt watched as he sucked it down, and then went after another, and then another. His mother chirped her approval, and the other two adults finished off the remaining bites. They all looked up at him.

"What? You want more? I'm sorry. You just ate it all. I can bring more this weekend if you'd like to make it a date." He reached out his hand hoping one of them would allow him to touch their nose again. To his surprise, the baby moved forward, chirped, and touched his nose to Matt's fingertips.

He laughed. "I'm going to call you George after a very curious monkey. What do you think?" The baby dolphin chirped repeatedly. His mother butted her head under his hand seeking attention. "You guys are pretty cool, you know that?"

In reply, the other two spun around and sloshed water at him with their tails. Matt sat covered in sea spray. He eyed the two devils. "Except for you two." He laughed when they began chattering in unison.

"Okay, come on over here." He reached his free hand out, and before he knew it, he was petting all four of them on their noses. "I'm Matt, by the way. In case you were wondering."

A strong feeling washed over him, a dizzying sense of deja vu. A face flashed in his mind, one that was laughing, surrounded by sea spray. It was a girl, but he couldn't make out her features. The sun was in his eyes, blurring his vision, hiding her face. All he could make out was dark hair and a gorgeous smile. He felt lightheaded and sat back down inside the boat. The waves kept him off-balance, and he listed sideways. He grabbed the side quickly and righted himself, panicked.

"What was that?" He looked at the four dolphins, who were watching him with what could only be described as concern. Matt picked up his canteen and guzzled down mouthfuls of water. He took a deep breath and wiped his lips with the back of his hand. "I'm okay, guys."

George chirped.

"It might just be a little too much sun. I waited a long time for you to show up, you know."

One after the other, the dolphins splashed water over Matt's head showering him with sea spray.

"Hey!" He shook his head. The breeze shifted and billowed out his shirt cooling his wet skin. "I don't know if you guys are trying to cool me down or just being smartasses."

The adults chirped. George came to the side again and peeked his nose over. Matt rubbed it.

"Okay. I'm going to take that as you guys being helpful. But I have to get home now. What do you think about meeting up again the day after tomorrow? I'll bring the squid."

Happy chortles sounded, and one after the other, they swam off.

George was the last to go. He swam in circles as Matt pulled anchor and grabbed the oars. He rowed north up the coast until he hit deeper water and then started the motor. For a time, his four new friends seemed to follow making sure he got back to his dock safely. It was an extraordinary day.

Chapter 10

Friday's class began with an announcement.

"We have a new teaching assistant joining us."

Mr. Jeffries indicated the tall, blonde-haired young woman standing off to the side of the room. She wore a stylish blue blazer over a white button-down shirt tucked into a navy-blue skirt that ended just above her knees. Her blouse strained a bit over her breasts, and her makeup was heavy, but she was stunning. Elizabeth noted that her classmate, Brett, was practically drooling, and he kept slapping his friend—whose name she learned was Carlos—on the arm.

Mr. Jeffries continued. "This is Angelica Mason, and she will be with us for the rest of the semester. Welcome her and don't give her a hard time or heads will roll," he said, half-jokingly.

Brett snorted and whispered, "I'd love to give her a *hard* time! Man, why can't she be our model?"

Carlos punched Brett in the shoulder. "Like you'd know what to do with that. Step aside, son. That one is all mine."

Elizabeth tried to hide her smile at their antics. *Boys,* she thought. *They're such clowns.*

"Prepare your palettes. Our model will be here in a few minutes. Continue to work on the impressions using form, lighting, and color. If you have any questions, raise your hand and I or Angelica will assist you."

Elizabeth poured thinner into her jar, and added more neutral tones along with some red, gold, and green to her palette. When she looked up again, the young man was standing on the dais, nude, and looking straight at her.

It was disconcerting. She coughed as the blush ran up her neck.

A smile spread across his lips.

A hand went up. "Mr. Jeffries? Is he going to smile like that now, because he wasn't smiling on Wednesday? It'll mess up my painting." A girl two easels to Elizabeth's left asked, clearly annoyed.

The instructor looked at the model, who quickly relaxed his face into a neutral expression.

"Matt, please refrain from improvising."

"Yes, sir," Matt answered, but there was a twinkle in his eyes as he looked just past Elizabeth.

So, his name is Matt.

Elizabeth began with light strokes creating the waves of his hair. *It fits him.* The corner of her lips lifted as she became lost in her own thoughts and the creative process.

Angelica walked slowly around the room behind each student checking out their works in progress. Finally, she came up behind Elizabeth, who was now drawing long lines to outline the body.

"That's very good. I think you've captured the physique exquisitely."

Elizabeth jumped. She turned and looked at the TA. "Thanks."

Angelica looked past her at Matt. Her eyes raked him from head to toe, and a cat-like smirk puckered her lush lips. Matt kept his gaze, for the most part, fixed on the window just behind Elizabeth. But every few minutes, that curious, green-eyed gaze would wander just a hair to the right and take in the pretty art student. When she turned to look at the new TA, the sun caught her features, blurring them just a little. His mind flashed back to the weird vision he had out on Tillamook Bay the day before. The two were eerily similar. Confusion clouded his thinking, but a sense of importance filled him, like he'd made the biggest discovery of his life.

The hour ticked by faster than expected. When Mr. Jeffries called time, he reached down to pick up his robe and disappeared down the hall to change back into his clothes. He dressed quickly, determined to meet this girl when she went to her car. He'd made a point of parking as close as possible that morning, finding a spot facing her bright yellow SmartBug. He lucked out in nabbing the space directly in front of hers.

Matt hoisted his backpack over his shoulder and ran out to his car. There, he waited, looking for all the world like he was just about to unlock his door. Minutes passed, and she hadn't yet appeared. He began to feel foolish when he caught sight of her out of the corner of his eye. She came bounding down the stairs, and across the lot, pulling out her keys as she drew nearer to her car.

Matt froze. He had no idea what to say. In his haste to get outside first, he hadn't planned this part out. His mind raced for something, anything relevant to start a conversation.

"Hi!"

He closed his eyes and sucked in a breath. *Hi? That's all you could come up with?* Matt shook his head, silently calling himself every kind of idiot.

Elizabeth looked up as she pulled her door open. The model named Matt stood watching her.

"Hi." She smiled tentatively.

He stood motionless and silent. That silence stretched out.

Thinking she must've misheard, Elizabeth shrugged, then slid into the driver's seat.

"Wait!" Matt walked over quickly, coming to a stop by her car.

"Yes?" Elizabeth waited.

"Sorry. I was wondering, well..." He looked away, shifting his weight from one foot to the other.

"Wondering what?"

He looked down and their eyes met. Stunned, he stared, unable to look away.

"I was wondering if maybe you'd like to join me for coffee...or lunch?"

This surprised her. "Me?"

He smiled. "Yeah, you and me." He glanced at his shoes, then back up at her. "What do you think?"

She blinked, unsure what to say. "We don't even know each other."

"Oh, yeah." He stuck his hand out. "I'm Matt. Matt McCandless. You've seen me naked."

Elizabeth choked, embarrassment heating her cheeks. Hesitantly, she reached out, and his large hand gently engulfed her smaller one. Sparks skipped over her skin, tingling pleasantly. Her eyes widened and looked straight into his, which were equally wide with shock.

"What was that?" she blurted.

Matt looked down at her delicate fingers resting in his hand. The heat between them spread throughout his entire body. He didn't want to let go. His green eyes lit up, and a slow smile spread across his face.

"Chemistry?"

Elizabeth blushed. Matt knelt next to her seat. "What's your name?"

"Elizabeth. Elizabeth Eaton." Her mouth felt dry, and her voice cracked.

Matt repeated her name. "Elizabeth."

Just the sound of it on his lips caused warmth to spread down to her belly.

"Elizabeth, would you have lunch with me?"

"Sure. I mean, yes, I guess that would be okay. Um, where?"

"Wherever you'd like to go." He still held her hand.

"There's a sandwich shop across the street," she suggested, glancing over at Souper Sandwiches.

"Okay." Matt stood, and still holding her hand, helped her out of her car.

"Uh...I need that." Elizabeth glanced at her hand.

"What?" He looked at their still-clasped hands, and then reluctantly let go. "Sorry." He stuck his hands in his pockets.

She reached in for her purse, then closed and locked the car door. Together, they made their way across the street. Inside, they found a table and sat down. It was a small, deli-style diner that catered to the college staff and students.

Elizabeth fidgeted. She glanced at Matt and noticed he was fidgeting too. She wondered if he might be as nervous as she was.

"I haven't eaten here. Is it any good?" He picked up two menus from the center of the table and handed her one.

"It's not bad. I've stopped in twice, but I ordered to go. This is the first time I've come inside to eat here otherwise."

"What do you recommend?" His green eyes watched her over the top of the menu.

"Um…I usually just grab a turkey with pesto on wheat."

Matt tossed the menu down. "Then two turkeys with pesto on wheat it is. I'll go order." He backed his chair up and stood. "What would you like to drink?"

"Lemonade?" Elizabeth shifted in her seat, not used to being waited on.

"You got it." Matt winked at her and walked to the counter.

She watched him go as she nervously readjusted her chair, then smoothed her hair.

Is this really happening? She watched him order their meal. Then she let her eyes roam over his hair. It was a little long, like he was overdue for a haircut, but she liked how it began to curl at the tips. Her fingers itched to touch those curls.

Lost in thought, she barely noticed when someone walked in until that person made their way to the counter. It was more accurate to say she sauntered up to the counter, and before the cups of lemonade were placed in his hands, Matt was being chatted up by the new teaching assistant from her art class.

Elizabeth watched in growing apprehension as the woman slowly moved in close to Matt, smiling up at him while she placed her hand on his arm. It was a flirtatious gesture. When he didn't back away, Elizabeth began to wonder if they already knew each other. Her body language indicated a familiarity that went beyond just acquaintances.

What in the world was going on?

Matt stood holding his and Elizabeth's drinks while Angelica backed him up against the counter. She was coming on strong, and with his hands full, and very little room to maneuver, he was having trouble putting her off and backing away. He could see Elizabeth out of the corner of his eye, and judging by the look on her face, she was getting entirely the wrong idea.

"I was impressed with you today. Have you modeled before? You were very professional considering the level of maturity coming from those kids." Angelica's hand continued to rest on his arm, gently squeezing his bicep.

Matt pulled his elbow back as fast as he could without spilling the drink in his hand.

"Yeah, thanks. No, it's my first gig, and most likely the last. But thanks." He tried to sidestep her.

"Wait. Where are you going? Have lunch with me. We can discuss maybe a new modeling job for you, say...at my place? Later?" Her eyes flashed and she arched her back causing the buttons on her blouse to strain across her cleavage.

"What? Uh, no. I'm here with someone." Matt scooted further away and pointed behind him.

"You are? Who?" Angelica looked around him, and then raised a perfectly arched eyebrow.

"With Elizabeth..." Matt turned and stopped talking. The table was empty, and Elizabeth was gone.

Stunned, he set the drinks on the counter and ran out of the restaurant. He was just in time to see a bright yellow SmartBug turn the corner and disappear from sight.

Angelica walked out behind him, a bag of sandwiches and two drinks in her hands.

"Looks like you got stood up." She held out a drink. "I grabbed your order. Seems a shame for it to go to waste," she said, her blue eyes looking up at him from beneath long, dark lashes.

Matt eyed the teaching assistant. He was sure seeing him talking to her was the reason Elizabeth left. He wanted to apologize and assure her there was nothing going on with the blonde TA, but he had no way of contacting her. He'd have to wait until their next class...and hope she would speak to him.

A hand tugged at his arm.

"Come back inside. No reason we can't enjoy lunch together. You can tell me all about this girl."

"Elizabeth," he mumbled.

"Who? Oh, yes. Elizabeth." Angelica's eyes narrowed. "From art class?" she asked.

Matt nodded. "Yeah."

The blonde TA bit her lip. "The dark-haired girl…"

He shrugged. "Uh huh. I'd only just asked her out." He glanced one last time at the now-empty street, disappointment reflected on his face.

Angelica watched him, a tight smile on her lips. "Well, if she's the type to just run off like that, I'd say you dodged a bullet." She patted his arm, her hand lingering. "Not a very nice thing to do to such a sweet guy," she added, her lashes fluttering. She nodded toward the diner. "Come on, Matt the model. There's a perfectly nice lady who really does want to have lunch with you." She tossed a saucy smile his way.

Matt sighed and looked at the woman holding his arm. He was aware she was flirting with him. And she really was beautiful in a rather overdone way, but he just couldn't switch gears like that. He reached up and gently disengaged her hand from his arm.

"Thanks, but I think I'll just head home. Keep the sandwiches," he said, and then waved as he walked back across the street.

Angelica stood, holding the bag, and watching him go. The smile on her lips disappeared, and a speculative glint lit her blue eyes.

As soon as he drove out of the parking lot, she dropped the bag of sandwiches into a waste bin and headed for her car. Thoughts of how best to lure the good-looking model away from an undeserving girl made the long drive home fly by.

Chapter 11

The week flew by in a flurry of activity. Elizabeth hardly noticed until Friday came around. She was just leaving work at the hospital, and she was still waffling over her dilemma. Go to art class and see Matt standing on the dais—naked—and try to paint him while ignoring what had happened or...skip it? She'd never skipped a class before, at least, not deliberately. Oh, she'd missed once because she'd been sick, but then, she'd called her professor and arranged to have the day's lesson sent by email. She had her homework completed and sent in before the next class. But this would be different. If she skipped out today, she'd miss valuable time working on her project with no way to make it up.

She stopped by her car, her fingers on the door handle. *Seeing Matt again will be awkward no matter if it's sooner or later*, she mused. But later sounded better, and she might be able to come in on Saturday morning to do some background work. That might make up for a missed hour.

Satisfied she'd at least dodged the awkwardness of seeing him for another week, Elizabeth smiled and pulled her cellphone from her pocket. She fired off a quick text to Mr. Jeffries explaining she had to work late and asked if she might be able to come in the next morning to work on her project.

The reply came back quickly, letting her know that would be okay, but not to make a habit of missing classes.

Happy with the outcome but cringing inwardly for both the lie and her own cowardice, Elizabeth assured her instructor that would not be the case and thanked him in a quick return text before sliding behind the wheel of her SmartBug. Now she had an entire afternoon to herself with nothing to do but think about the guy she'd just gone out of her way to avoid. She headed home, stopping to pick up lunch along the way.

After tossing down the last of her submarine sandwich and chips, she pulled out her sketch pad and charcoals and began working. She hadn't known what she was going to sketch when she began, but before long, the lines and shadows took on a familiar masculine shape. She stopped and stared at her work.

It was Matt, and yet it wasn't. Still, the face emerging from the paper was one she was sure she knew. Frustrated, she flipped the page over and tried again. After an hour, the same face, the Matt/not Matt face, stared back at her from the pad. The eyes teased and the hint of a smile at the corners of his lips promised laughter. The hairstyle was a bit different, shorter, and with a bit more curl, and the shoulders were a tad broader. In all, a good effort, except her charcoal wielding fingers kept revealing someone slightly different than the image held in her mind. She was both intrigued and annoyed.

Still, she had something she could work with in the morning, that was all that mattered. She placed the sketches in her pad and put away her pencils and charcoals. Once that task was complete, Elizabeth pulled out her cellphone and typed a quick text.

Movie tonight?

She waited for a reply.

Can't. Dinner with Jack. How about tomorrow night?

Jack was Lacy's latest romantic interest, and so far, seemed like a decent guy.

Okay. How about seven, and dinner after?

You got it, came the reply.

Smiling, Elizabeth headed to her room to pick out an outfit for a Saturday night out.

She'd been so busy with work and school that weeks had gone by without any girl time with her best friend Lacy. The two had been thick as thieves since high school, and the best part about their friendship was the fact that no matter what was going on in their lives, when one called the other to get together, they picked up right where they left off. And Elizabeth had a lot to tell Lacy. After all, it wasn't every day a guy walked into her life, much less one not wearing any clothes.

She giggled, anticipating Lacy's reaction. She knew already that her friend would demand details. Elizabeth's cheeks heated at the thought of Matt's naked body. Even though things hadn't worked out, that he and the teaching assistant had something going on, it didn't negate the fact that she'd found him quite attractive. Maybe in another life, she thought, as she changed into fresh jeans, a bright pink sweater, and grabbed her favorite pink high top sneakers. The truth was that the other woman was a big red flag, and Elizabeth didn't want to get enmeshed in a bad situation. While she'd really like to meet a nice guy and fall in love, she didn't want to get hurt, and a guy dating multiple women had heartbreaker written all over him.

No, Matt McCandless was great on canvas, but in the real world, he came with strings attached. Lacy would enjoy the story, and Elizabeth would enjoy the company of her best friend over a movie and dinner after. Then, tomorrow, she would catch up on her art project, and hopefully, her life would get back on track.

Elizabeth grabbed her purse and keys and headed out the door, the concerns of her heart light and her worries fading.

Chapter 12

Matt sat anchored in the bay, the choppy waves tossing the boat to and fro. A full bag of chum threatened to overturn from his tackle box, evidence that George and his friendly family of striped dolphins had either moved on or were steering clear of the bay for now. Either way, it left him with a lot of time to think and a smelly bag of fish parts that would only stink more as the day wore on. He picked it up and dumped it overboard, rinsing the bag before placing it back inside the tackle box.

In the distance, clouds gathered, darkening the western horizon. They were the perfect metaphor for his mood. He'd hoped to see Elizabeth today and clear up whatever it was that made her run away from their date. He wasn't even sure it could be called a date, but it was something. At least, it was to him. Then the teaching assistant, Angelica, came in and had come on strong. He could only imagine how that looked from where Elizabeth was sitting. It was just a misunderstanding all the way around, and he'd wanted the chance to explain, and to try again. But Elizabeth was a no-show to class. He found himself standing there naked for an hour, lost in thought the entire time. Even so, he'd been aware of one thing; Angelica. The teaching assistant seemed to be making an effort to stay in his line of sight, casting what could only be described as a hungry look his way, lashes fluttering. Any other time, he might've been flattered, but in this case, he was annoyed.

Her persistence meant he would need to tell her, in no uncertain terms, that he wasn't interested. Those types of conversations were awkward as heck, and he didn't like hurting anyone's feelings. Maybe he could put it off a little longer, just avoid her.

At the end of the hour, he'd picked up his robe, ready to make a quick getaway to the men's room but she stood by the door, blocking his exit.

"Great job today."

Matt nodded. "Thanks."

He kept his head down and tried to go around her.

She let him pass but stepped into the hall behind him.

"Busy later? Maybe we could grab dinner?"

Matt sighed. He glanced her way, noticing how her fingers played with the top button on her blouse, a deliberate move to draw his eye. There was no doubt that Angelica was a pretty woman. But she wasn't Elizabeth. The two were as different as night and day. Angelica was bold, obvious, and sophisticated. Elizabeth was softer, sweeter, and understated in a way that was sexier than any woman he'd ever laid eyes on. When he looked at Angelica, he knew exactly who she was. He didn't even have to guess.

Elizabeth, however, was different. She was shy, and a bit mysterious. She wasn't the type to put herself out there for everyone. No. She was the kind of girl whose trust must be earned, whose secrets would only be revealed when she felt safe to do so. He wanted to earn her trust and be the guy she felt safe around. That meant being crystal clear now.

He cleared his throat.

"Sorry, Angelica, but I can't. You see, Elizabeth—"

"Oh, will you be seeing her later?"

Mr. Jeffries poked his head out the door, interrupting them.

"Remind her that the classroom will only be open from nine until noon tomorrow. Oh, and to not make a habit of skipping class. I understand about work, but if she gets behind, she'll have to make it up next semester." The teacher glanced Angelica's way. "I left the graded tests from Wednesday's class on the desk. Enter those scores in before you leave today."

Mr. Jeffries waited for Angelica to return to the classroom before patting Matt on the back.

"You're doing a great job. See you next week."

Matt nodded, then ran to the men's room to change, relieved to have escaped that awkward conversation with Angelica, at least, for now. And now he knew why Elizabeth had been absent. Work. He'd been worried she was trying to avoid him, and he still had some explaining to do, but hope filled him. He might still have a chance.

That was the thought that lifted his spirit all the way home and during his jaunt out into the bay. But when the dolphins didn't show up, and the clouds began to gather, his mood took a decided downward turn. The problem was still there. Elizabeth had run from him, and Angelica was still pursuing him.

But now he knew where one of them would be tomorrow morning, and she was the only one that mattered.

He cast his gaze out over the bay one last time.

"Well, George, you missed out on some good chum. Maybe next time. Wish me luck, little buddy. I have to see about a girl and do some serious explaining."

He pulled anchor and grabbed the oars, steering the boat back to deeper water before switching to the motor for the rest of the ride home.

That night, the skies let loose a torrent. Lightning flashed, illuminating the walls inside Matt's childhood bedroom. Not much had changed in this room since he'd gone off to college. Posters of his favorite bands hung on the walls and football trophies and science fair prize ribbons decorated the top shelf of a bookcase containing classic titles mixed with textbooks on marine biology and How-to's for hobbies such as woodworking and boat building. Thunder shook the double-paned glass in the only window facing out toward the bay, but Matt didn't hear any of it. He was lost inside a familiar dream.

"Well I'll be..." He let his gaze roam over her face.

"What?" the pretty girl before him asked.

He smiled. "I'm the first guy to tell you how beautiful you are. That's kind of special."

Elizabeth swallowed, or was it someone else? Her face seemed so familiar. He was sure it was her, his love. His girl. First, he'd called her pretty, which was the world's biggest understatement, and now he told her she was beautiful. She stood before him with her mouth agape, her lips forming an inviting 'O'.

His eyes dropped to those lips. Soft, naturally pink, and free of any lipstick. Without any doubt, he knew she'd never been kissed. The temptation to add another first to her list drew him closer. Their noses touched and he tilted his head, angling closer. The space of a single breath separated them. He sank his fingers into her silky soft hair, gently caressing as he held her face still. He'd never wanted to kiss anyone in his life as badly as he wanted to kiss her at this moment.

He felt hot, and excited. His heart was racing. He could almost hear the hum between their bodies. The kiss began gently, slowly. One, two, and then three soft kisses landed upon her sweet lips. Then he kissed her again, and she sighed. As soon as he heard that sound of pleasure, he deepened the kiss. His tongue ran along her lower lip, and dipped inside, tasting her innocence. In that moment, everything changed. His entire being felt as if it had burst into flame, hot and needy. His hands slid down her neck and shoulders roaming over her back and bringing her up against him in a way that lit his whole body on fire. It was incredible.

He was lost in the wonder that was Melissa...no...Elizabeth! His body was responding to her softness, and there was a primal feeling that she was his, only his, and no one had ever kissed her before this day. He would always be her first kiss. Then he realized he'd be another first if he didn't stop. But it felt so right...

Thunder boomed, rattling the window once again, and Matt's eyes popped open. He stared around the room, momentarily disoriented.

Where am I?

Piece by piece, his memory unlocked, and he remembered he was home, in his old bedroom for the weekend. And the clearer the present became, the less he recalled the dream, but his body remembered. Need still surged through him as he flipped over and punched the pillow, willing his wayward parts to calm down so he could go back to sleep and find the elusive beauty whose face he could no longer see clearly, but was sure he knew.

Elizabeth tossed and turned, her legs kicking the covers off. Air cooled her skin, but inside, passion burned.

Oh, my God! This is torture. Why would anyone want to do this? Back up! No, come closer. I don't know what to do! All these thoughts ran through her mind at the speed of light, and while she tried to make sense out of it all, his lips found hers, and the world exploded, ceasing to exist outside of the two of them. Every part of her body felt overheated and sensitive. Where she felt he was too close before, now he was not close enough. His hands slid down her neck and shoulders roaming over her back and bringing her up against him in a way that made her feel boneless. It was wonderful. It answered so many questions she'd had before. It was terrifying, too, because she felt so many things at once, she didn't know what to do or how to react. All she could manage was to allow herself to be swept along on this hot current of desire.

He would always be her first kiss. But there was someone else between them, someone tearing them apart, even if her body screamed for her to forget about that and stay in the moment. Her mind was stronger, and she pulled away. She stood, stunned, panting and staring at his handsome, familiar face, surprised at herself, but confused...

Lightning lit the night sky, illuminating the walls of her bedroom where it stole through the cracks of the slatted blinds. It was dark again in the blink of an eye as thunder rolled, rumbling like a freight train.

Elizabeth blinked back tears, awash in unexplainable sorrow. Even as desire still simmered beneath the surface of her air-cooled skin, her heart was breaking, and she didn't know why. All she knew was something was missing. Or someone.

The words, *"All you had to do was say yes. You didn't have to fall for me, too,"* echoed in her mind as most of the dream faded.

She sniffed, staring at the ceiling. "What in the world?" she whispered.

Elizabeth took several deep breaths, and her racing heart calmed. She rolled over, hugging her pillow for comfort. A few stray tears rolled down her cheeks as she closed her eyes and let sleep wash over her again. This time, it was peaceful.

Chapter 13

Saturday dawned a foggy and overcast day, but otherwise quiet. The rain had moved on leaving the ground soaked and some roads impassable.

Elizabeth took her time getting to campus and parked her yellow SmartBug near the art building. Inside, the only people she came across were a couple of other students working on a project two classrooms down and the janitor. She entered her own classroom and went about setting up her station. Soon, she was lost in thought as she worked from her sketches the day before to bring more depth and definition to her painting.

The tip of the brush glided over the edge of the jaw, providing shadow, and adding the illusion of strength. She stared at the contrast with the highlight over the cheekbones and the jut of the chin. It looked right, but it was his eyes which drew her attention. Switching brushes, Elizabeth chose a finer point and began mixing her colors. A deep emerald and a lighter yellow green.

She began with the irises and the yellow green. Stroke by stroke and layer by layer, she added in the darker emerald, and then flecks of gold before switching to the contrasting dark shades for the pupils and defining lines and edges. Before long, his eyes were staring back at her.

"That's kind of freaky, staring at myself."

Elizabeth yelped and dropped her paintbrush.

Matt bent to pick it up.

"Sorry, I didn't mean to scare you."

A muttered curse slipped past her lips, and she turned to face the person she'd tried so hard to avoid.

She didn't know what to say. Embarrassment and irritation warred with the oddly giddy excitement of seeing the handsome young man from her painting standing before her. As their eyes connected, she realized she could never in a million years capture the sensation that zinged through her being and vibrated in her very soul when he looked at her like he was looking at her right now.

"What are you doing here?" she asked.

Matt handed her the brush.

"Not helping, it seems," he joked.

She took the brush from his hand, their fingers touching briefly. But that was all it took to send heat rushing up her slender neck and settling beneath her porcelain skin.

A small smile tugged his lips as the roses bloomed on her cheeks. He hoped it was because of the crazy electricity sizzling between them and not because she was mad. Either way, he was mesmerized by her beauty. He took a chance.

"Um, well, your teacher said you'd be in today to make up for missing yesterday's class. I was worried you might be sick or something and wanted to make sure you were okay. Plus, Mr. Jeffries said to remind you not to miss any more classes…"

Elizabeth stared at him, surprised.

"You were worried about me?"

Her words cut through his rambling.

"Well, yeah. I mean, after you left our lunch date, I didn't know if you were okay, or if I'd done something wrong, or said something wrong." He stopped and looked at her. "What did I do wrong? Whatever it was, I'm so sorry. I didn't mean it. I'd never want to hurt your feelings, not ever."

And there it was, the question she didn't really know how to answer. How does one explain feeling like a third wheel, or worse, feeling jealous when they've barely spent any time together? It was embarrassing.

She shuffled her feet and took a moment to lay the brush down on the table.

Clearing her throat, she hoped an answer that wouldn't humiliate her forever would magically find its way to her tongue.

"You seemed...busy at the time." She kept her eyes cast down, afraid he'd see right through her vague words.

Matt slid his hands in his pockets. "Busy how? I was there with you and only getting us lunch."

"I know, but..." Elizabeth felt her face flame hotter.

"But...what? You mean Angelica? The TA?" he asked.

She coughed once. "She seemed very familiar with you."

A chuckle escaped his lips, and then he laughed straight out.

"I barely know her. Just met her here, same as you, my first day modeling for this class."

She gave him a sharp look. "Then why was she touching you like that?"

He shook his head. "Believe me, I was asking myself the same thing. I tried to get away from her as fast as I could, but when I turned around, you were already gone."

"So, you aren't seeing her?"

"No. No, I'm not." Matt smiled and ran a hand through his hair. "Elizabeth, I'm not the kind of guy who messes around like that. I don't know what she wanted. I just know that it was you I wanted to be with, and I'm really sorry if you thought otherwise. Do you think maybe we could try again? Like, maybe have dinner with me tonight?"

He was doing it again, looking at her in that way that made her feel all gooey inside. He wasn't dating the teaching assistant. Even better, he wanted to date her. And he'd gone out of his way to find her and apologize. How could she say no? And then she remembered.

"No, not tonight."

Matt blinked, disappointment in his green eyes. He backed up a step.

"Okay. I get it. I messed up—"

She reached out and grabbed his hand. "No, no. That's not what I mean. It's just that..."

The electricity sparking up her arm and zipping through her body caused her tongue to short circuit.

He stopped moving, equally stunned. "Just that...what?"

She struggled for air, and then sucked in a deep breath. "Just that I already have plans tonight."

His face fell again. "Oh."

She grinned, seeing he'd misunderstood her again. "With my best friend, Lacy. We're going to see a movie."

Relief washed over him, and the twinkle returned to his eyes. "How about tomorrow afternoon? Late lunch? Early dinner?"

"Late lunch sounds nice."

Matt entwined his fingers with hers enjoying the crazy sensations humming between them.

"Okay. Around three? I'll pick you up."

His thumb caressed the inside of her wrist, and her heart skipped a beat.

"Guess you'll need my address," she said, her voice catching.

"Guess I will," he replied.

Time stopped as they stood there, caught in the magic of the moment.

He tore his eyes away from her beautiful brown ones and glanced at the painting of himself and then at the table where a sketch pad lay open revealing an uncanny drawing of himself. The idea that she'd been thinking of him as she drew each line made him smile.

"Are you finished for the day? I could walk you out."

Elizabeth's eyes followed his line of sight to the sketch book, and she blushed all over again. Now he knew she'd been thinking about him over the last few days. She gently pulled her hand away and began packing up her things, closing the sketch pad first before turning her attention to the paint brushes.

"Yes, I think so. Just let me clean up and put these away."

She set about soaking her brushes in mineral spirits and wiping away the excess paint before taking them over to the sink and rinsing them clean. Once she put everything back on her table and pulled the sheet cloth down over her canvas, she picked up her backpack and turned to Matt.

He had a piece of paper in one hand and a pen in the other.

"Your address, my lady, please?" He wiggled his brows, mischief in his eyes.

Elizabeth bit her lip to keep from laughing and she quickly jotted down the information.

Tucking the pen and paper in his shirt pocket, Matt reached for her hand once again and led them out of the classroom, and down the hall to the exit.

She watched as they exited the classroom, both too enamored of the other to notice her approaching from the other end of the hall. She thought about calling out to Matt, but the couple disappeared through the exit leaving Angelica standing by the classroom door, seething. She'd come in under the pretense of logging in grades for Mr. Jeffries. The real reason, of course, was that she'd hoped to run into Matt. Knowing Elizabeth would be making up missed class time on Saturday and seeing the sexy male model's interest when Mr. Jeffries mentioned it had set the wheels in her mind spinning. She couldn't be sure, but she felt reasonably confident he'd show up. She'd planned then to be here, but she had no idea what time and had miscalculated.

She'd missed her chance and would have to wait until Monday.

Frustrated, she entered the room and slammed her purse and folders down on the desk. She stood tapping her high-heeled shoe on the tile. Looking around the room, her eyes fell on the model's dais in the center, and then she glanced at the easels, all of them covered to protect the works in progress. She stared hard at Elizabeth's. Before she knew what she was doing, she'd walked across the room to her station.

There, she whipped the drop cloth aside and gasped. The girl really did have talent. The green eyes gazing back at her were most definitely Matt's, but at the same time, there was something more.

Her heart rate increased, and a warm rush of blood flowed through her body. There was something about the painting, something that spoke to her. Angelica reached out to touch the side of his face but stopped. Emotions welled from deep within. First awe, then sorrow, and finally, rage. She slashed out with her sharp fingernails, clawing lines through the eyes of the young man in the painting repeatedly, tears running down her cheeks as she snarled, *"You will not leave me for her!"*

Her fury drove her until the sound of footsteps in the hall brought her back from the brink. Angelica backed away from the easel and saw the damage she'd done. The painting was destroyed. Nothing but claw marks and muddied oils were visible anymore. Shaking, she quickly recovered the desecrated canvas and went to the sink to wash her hands. The cold water cooled her anger, but her nails were ruined. She glanced over her shoulder at the open doorway and beyond to the empty hall. Whoever had been out there was already gone. Drying her hands on a paper towel, she went to retrieve her purse, leaving the folders behind as she dashed out of the classroom and ran to her car. It would not do for her to be caught at the scene of the crime.

As she drove out of the parking lot, she began to relax. A small smile tugged her red painted lips. No one saw her. No one would know. And come Monday, she would see the horrified look on that prim face when Elizabeth arrived in class and uncovered what was left of her precious portrait.

Chapter 14

Her hands trembled. Her heart pounded. But despite her nerves, Elizabeth was on cloud nine. Matt showed up at three on the dot outside her apartment door with a bouquet of pink peonies. It was the sweetest gesture she could remember outside of her prom date in high school presenting her with a corsage of white roses. The difference between then and now, however, was how both made her feel. Brad was her first date. It was an odd thing to admit that she hadn't dated like other girls her age until the nice boy in her algebra class had asked, but it was true, nonetheless. She liked Brad, and they had a good time at the dance, but after that night, and the less than earth-shattering goodnight kiss, they decided to remain friends. Now, the boy on her doorstep presenting flowers wasn't a boy, but a handsome young man, and all they'd done so far was hold hands, yet her knees went weak. If he kissed her later, she feared she might faint...and that would be too embarrassing.

"Hope you like them," he said, watching her intently.

She smiled. No, more like she grinned like a loon. Couldn't help herself.

"I love them! Pink is my favorite color," she said, inviting him in as she turned to enter the kitchen.

Matt eyed the blush-pink blouse paired with figure-hugging jeans with appreciation. She wore bright pink heels that made her legs look even longer. His gaze traveled back up to her hair, loosely piled atop her head with a few wispy curls hanging down. His heart flipped in his chest.

"I see that," he murmured.

Elizabeth reached into the cabinet and pulled out a vase while Matt leaned against the counter. As he watched, she filled it with water from the sink and placed the bouquet inside, arranging the peonies.

"They're so pretty," she said, then leaned over to smell their fragrance.

Matt sighed. "Sure are...uh, is," he added, straightening. "So, are you ready?"

"Yes. Uh, hope I'm dressed properly. You didn't say where we were going." She glanced down at her outfit before taking in his. He wore jeans, as well, but with a blue collared Polo shirt that brought out the green in his eyes, reminding her of the ocean.

"You're perfect," he replied, then cleared his throat. "I made a reservation for us. Not fancy, but really nice. I think you'll like it. At least, I hope you do."

The way he looked at her had her whole body humming a happy tune.

"I'm sure I will. Let me grab my purse and keys." She picked up the items and led the way to the door, locking it on the way out. "I'm ready."

Matt offered his hand. Elizabeth let her fingers slide between his, feeling the warm, electric fuzzy bees swarm over her skin. He smiled at her as they descended the stairs to the parking lot below. The trembling in her hands returned, but this time, it flooded her whole body, and it felt...good.

Matt caressed her hand with his thumb, enjoying the blush on her cheeks. Pink. Her favorite color, and now his, too.

Giardino was packed with Sunday afternoon diners, but that wasn't a problem for Matt and Elizabeth. The Italian eatery had their table ready on the terrace. Replicas of Italy's greatest statues were placed around the garden-styled terrace surrounded by lush greenery and flowering plants. In the center of the outdoor dining area was a miniaturized version of the Piazza del Popolo's Neptune Fountain. As the water burbled, a trio of musicians played traditional Italian music from a small corner stage just inside the restaurant. As impressive as it was, the atmosphere was relaxed and the dining casual.

A waiter filled their water glasses and informed them of the day's specials. Elizabeth ordered the Spinach and Ricotta Lasagna while Matt chose the Spaghetti Carbonara.

Over warm rosemary bread fresh from the oven and a simple seasoned olive oil for dipping, they got to know each other better, each asking a question in turn.

"Have you always wanted to be an artist?" he asked.

Elizabeth took a bite of bread and chewed thoughtfully.

"I guess so. When I was little, I took pictures with my dad's old cell phone. Lots of pictures. But I found myself looking at them more and more, wondering about the shapes, the lighting, and the colors, and how they all came together to create those pictures. I started out with crayons, trying to copy what I took pictures of. After a while, I got better at it and my grandmother gifted me my first set of art paints when I turned eleven. It just kind of went from there."

"Is that what you want to do then? Be a famous painter?"

She smiled. "I don't know about famous, but it would be nice to be able to sell my paintings."

He looked surprised.

"You haven't yet? Why not?"

She giggled. "Because I haven't tried?"

Matt looked around the terrace filled with sculptures, then inside at the walls where several paintings hung.

"Your work should be on those walls right now," he pointed.

"What?" Elizabeth replied, glancing at the interior paintings. "No way. I'm not that good."

"Yes, you are. I've seen your work, remember? Definitely as good, if not better. I mean, you've made me look like a model."

She laughed outright. "You ARE a model! And I just paint what I see."

"Well, you're seeing more than is here, I think. I mean, it looks like me, but like a better me."

"I don't think it's possible to see more," she said, blushing.

"Well," he began, then stopped. The beautiful pinkening of her cheeks stole the words from his lips and sent a jolt through him. He knew what she meant, even in jest, but the realization that she was, in this moment, thinking about him standing on a dais in the middle of the classroom, naked, had an odd effect on his ability to form any other thoughts.

The waiter returned with their order.

"The lasagna for you," he said, placing the plate before Elizabeth, "and the carbonara for you, sir," he added, setting the dish in front of Matt.

After adding fresh Parmesan to both at their requests, the waiter left them to enjoy their meal.

"And what about you? Do you want to be a professional model?"

Matt chuckled. "No, no. It's just a job. Seemed like an easy gig that pays well, and it fits in between my classes. What I want to do is become an ecologist with a secondary study as an environmental specialist. We've made some strides in protecting the environment, but we still have a long way to go."

"That's amazing." Elizabeth looked at Matt through new eyes. He wasn't just some handsome model, but someone who cared deeply about the world around him. And he was nice. He'd gone out of his way to make their date special but not overwhelming, and had picked the perfect place. She looked around the terrace garden. It was beautiful. The music set the mood, the food was incredible, and the company was more than she ever could have hoped.

"You think so?" he asked, his green eyes searching hers.

Elizabeth set down her fork and reached across the table, taking his hand.

"Yes, I really do. You want to make a difference, one that helps everyone. I think you're a good person, Matt McCandless."

Hearing her speak his full name sent warmth coursing through his body. A slow smile spread across his lips as he absently caressed her wrist with his thumb.

"I think you're amazing too."

Elizabeth's heart stopped, then beat again with the force of a drum. Her mouth went dry, and her limbs felt boneless. *How did he do that?*

She licked her lips and stuttered, "But you don't even know me..."

"I like what I know so far. And I want to know more about you, that is, if you'll let me."

She glanced at him, shyly.

"I'd like that."

Those three simple words sent Matt over the moon. He lifted her hand and placed a soft kiss on her knuckles.

The heat from his lips seared her skin and warmed her in places she wasn't prepared to acknowledge in a public setting.

He seemed to understand and, with a knowing smile, released her hand and asked if the lasagna was good. She shared a bite with him, and the rest of their date was spent in light conversation that she couldn't even remember anything about except that it was fun, and they laughed, and they got to know each other a little bit better. But she did remember the end of the date.

When he walked her to her door, Matt McCandless kissed her. It wasn't at all like the kiss from her prom date, Brad. Matt's kiss took her breath away. From the moment his lips touched hers, an overpowering current of desire zinged through her body, igniting every nerve, and setting her pulse to pounding. And when his tongue teased hers, the world exploded in light and color and sound. She desperately wanted to be closer to him. The fire burning between them made her ache with need, and she didn't know what to do. Matt pulled away first, but only enough to breathe. His eyes held hers, filled with passion and wonder. Her own reflected those same emotions, and they stood there, arms wrapped around each other, bodies pressed tightly together, catching their breath, suspended in the magic of the moment.

For Elizabeth, it was an awakening. For Matt, a revelation.

"See you Monday?" he asked, reluctant to let go.

She nodded and whispered, "Yes. Monday."

He dropped one last, soft kiss upon her lips.

"Sweet dreams," he murmured, then released her and walked down the stairs, glancing over his shoulder one last time.

She watched him go, knowing full well she would indeed be having sweet dreams this night.

Chapter 15

Elizabeth dashed across the parking lot, her pink sneakers pounding the pavement. She was late. Only two minutes, but she hated being the reason class would be disrupted, and she'd already missed the previous Friday. Still, the fender bender between the two cars in front of her had snarled traffic until police showed up and directed the waylaid drivers around the scene of the accident. She'd attempted to make up for lost time by pushing the speed limit, but after witnessing an accident, she didn't want to be the next statistic.

She bounded up the stairs and tried to quietly duck in through the open door of the classroom only to find yet more drama. All the other students were crowding around Mr. Jeffries, Dean Allen, the art department head, two campus security guards, and...the janitor? Elizabeth halted her stride and tried to see what was going on. That's when she noticed they were all standing around her workstation. And that's when they noticed her.

"Elizabeth, come here, please," Mr. Jeffries said.

Dread filled her gut as she approached. For the life of her, Elizabeth couldn't fathom what in the world she'd done, but with both the dean and security standing by, it had to be bad.

She stopped next to her easel and looked from the guards to the dean, and then to her instructor, eyes wide.

"Yes, sir?" She swallowed.

Mr. Jeffries' lips tightened, and his expression was inscrutable.

"There's been an incident," he began, then looked at her canvas.

Confused, Elizabeth blinked and then turned, her eyes following his.

Her jaw dropped. Her gut clenched, and the breath whooshed from her lungs.

"What happened?" she squeaked. "Who did this?" Tears sprang forth, blurring the vision of destruction before her.

"That's why everyone is here," Mr. Jeffries began, indicating Dean Allen, the security guards, and the janitor.

"I don't understand…" she whispered.

The dean stepped forward. "Mister Jimenez brought it to our attention," he said, gesturing toward the old janitor.

"Saw her do it, then she ran out," he said. The janitor's eyes were sympathetic.

"What? Who?"

Mr. Jeffries explained. "Mr. Jimenez informed the dean's office. We've seen the closed-circuit footage thanks to campus security. There is no question she is terminated as of now, and she will be escorted off campus when she shows up, but Elizabeth, we really think you need to call the police. What has happened here was no accident. For some reason, Angelica has targeted you and this act of violence suggests she means you harm."

Angelica.

Angelica, the teaching assistant, destroyed her painting. And they'd caught it on camera.

"When did this happen?"

Mr. Jimenez spoke. "Right after you left on Saturday. The other gal came in and I heard her screaming. I came to the door and peeked in, worried someone was hurt, and she was slashing the painting. Looked kinda crazy too. I went to call the campus police immediately. By the time they arrived, she was gone. Everything looked normal here, but when they checked the cameras, they saw what she did and took it to the dean. I'm so sorry."

"But...why? Why would she do this?"

Her instructor and the dean both shrugged. The janitor looked down, then said, "She sounded pissed about the boy. She screamed, "you won't take him from me again."

Again?

Just then, the "boy" in question walked into the classroom wearing his robe. He stopped when he saw the group of people gathered around Elizabeth.

She looked at him and the dam burst. Tears streamed unchecked down her cheeks.

Alarmed, Matt ran to her, pulling her into his arms. Then he saw what was left of her painting.

"What in the hell?"

"It was Angelica," she sniffed.

"I think we need to cancel class today, folks," Mr. Jeffries announced. "We'll meet again on Wednesday." As the other students packed up and filed out, he turned to Matt. "We were just telling Elizabeth that we think she needs to report this to the police. And she shouldn't be alone, not until they find Miss Mason. She hasn't shown up yet today."

Matt nodded, then looked at Elizabeth. "He's right," he said, glancing at the shredded canvas. "I mean, I thought she was aggressive at the sandwich shop, and even when she stopped me in the hall the other day, but I had no idea."

"Has she been harassing you, Matt?" Mr. Jeffries asked.

Matt shook his head. "She tried to hit on me, asked me out, but I..." he paused. "Well, I started to tell her no, but then you came out and asked me if I was going to see Elizabeth this past weekend, so I guess I never actually said it."

Dean Allen's expression grew worried. "A university employee harassing a student is serious business. It's becoming clearer that this is a stalking situation. I'll need you both to come to my office. I'll call in the local police, so you can file a complaint with them as well. I suggest a restraining order, Miss Eaton, for your protection."

Elizabeth gasped. The situation was growing more dire by the minute, and she didn't know what to do.

"He's right. Don't worry, though. I won't leave your side."

"You should file one as well, son," the dean said.

"Me?" Matt asked, surprised.

"Yes, you. Miss Mason's advances have been rejected by you and she's clearly blaming Miss Eaton. She might try to harm both of you. I'll expect you in my office immediately. Get changed," he said to Matt, "and escort Miss Eaton over. We'll get this sorted."

The dean and the security guards left. The janitor followed. Inside the classroom, Mr. Jeffries patted Elizabeth's shoulder.

"It's going to be okay. Don't worry about your painting. I'll give you plenty of time to redo the project. None of this was your fault. Just take care of your safety. That's what's important right now." He turned to Matt. "Watch over her. These things don't just fizzle out. It'll take some time."

Matt nodded. "I will." He reached up to tuck a lock of Elizabeth's hair behind her ear. "I'll just go get dressed. Stay here with Mr. Jeffries. I'll be right back and then we'll head over to Dean Allen's office."

She nodded and watched him go.

The day, which had dawned bright and full of hope, had turned dark and dangerous. She didn't know what to make of it all, and if she was honest, she'd admit out loud she was terrified. And angry. Elizabeth looked again at the ruined canvas. Only unbridled rage could do that kind of damage. And if Angelica could do that to her painting, what might she do if she came face to face with the blonde, now ex-TA? She swallowed hard, her body now trembling in shock. The adrenaline that had been coursing through her had subsided, leaving her with the shakes as an eerie calmness settled over her being. She lowered the backpack slung over her shoulder to the floor and sat on the stool to wait for Matt. Since she'd met him, everything had changed. Most of it was for the better. But this part…this part scared her. When would the scary part end?

Matt returned, as promised, and they met with the dean and local police. Within a few hours, all the necessary paperwork was filed, and the dean dismissed them both for the rest of the week until Angelica Mason could be served both orders of protection and their safety on campus ensured.

"What do we do now?" Elizabeth asked as they exited the building.

Matt squeezed her hand. "Go home, I suppose," he replied.

She stopped on the steps. "I'm afraid."

Her jaw quivered and the hand he still held trembled.

"What can I do?" he asked.

Her big, brown eyes, usually so calm and sure, peeked up at him filled with fear and uncertainty.

"Stay with me."

Her words were whispered, but he heard them loud and clear.

"I have a better idea," he said, thinking fast.

"What's that?"

"Well, we have a week off. How about you come stay with me at my parents' place? They have plenty of room. Then I can take you out on my boat."

Her eyes lit up. "You have a boat?"

"I do. Just a small one, but if we're lucky, I can introduce you to George."

"George?" she asked.

He smiled. "You'll see. That is, if you say yes."

"But I still have work. I don't know…" she said, chewing her lip.

"Is there anyone else who can cover for you?" he asked.

"Yes, but I hate to put anyone in a bind."

He nodded. "I get it, but under the circumstances, I think they'd understand. Give them a call and explain what's going on, see what they say."

"I suppose I could. But I don't want to impose on your parents."

"Trust me, you wouldn't be."

Elizabeth bit her lip, then agreed. "Okay. I mean, if your parents don't mind. I would feel safer, at least, until this is over."

Matt grinned, thrilled at the idea of spending the week with her. "Great! Make your call first, and then let's drop your car off, grab your things, then I'll grab mine, and then we'll head out to Tillamook."

Chapter 16

The hour and a half drive out to his parents' house in Tillamook was usually made in silence, or listening to his favorite music, but today, the miles flew by in a joyful whirl. Matt couldn't stop beaming. They talked about everything from childhood memories to the latest movies. What they didn't talk about was Angelica. He'd deliberately steered their conversations away from unpleasantness. Elizabeth didn't deserve what that woman had done to her painting, and the last thing he wanted was to see the clouds return to her beautiful eyes. He much preferred the smile on her lips.

They were nearly there. Matt knew his mom and dad would be waiting with the spare bedroom already made up for their unexpected guest. He'd called ahead while Elizabeth packed a bag and explained. Always the mother hen, his mom was the first to agree with the plan. She was also excited that her son was bringing a girl home, firing off questions and asking all about Elizabeth while his dad chuckled in the background and told his wife to calm down and not scare the poor girl off with her enthusiasm.

As soon as he pulled into the gravel driveway, Tom and Mary McCandless were there, standing on the front porch, welcoming smiles on their faces. Their home was the last one on a dead-end street that overlooked the bay. With only three other houses on Marine Street, the setting was ideal. Matt's parents bought the house twenty-two years ago with help from his grandfather, Bob McCandless. It was his grandparents' wedding gift to a much younger Tom and Mary. Baby Matthew came along almost two years later. He grew up playing in the bay in his backyard, swimming, fishing, and then boating. It was a happy childhood that inspired him to pursue a career in environmental studies. He couldn't wait to share it all with Elizabeth.

Next to him in the car, Elizabeth stopped talking and stared out the windshield as Matt parked in the driveway. Her good mood slipped a notch as uncertainty wiggled its way in. Matt noticed and reached over, taking her hand in his and giving it a squeeze.

"Don't worry. They don't bite."

She chuckled at his choice of words.

"Are you sure? What if they don't like me? Maybe I should get a hotel room..."

"Absolutely not. It's going to be fine; I promise. Mom will smother you with mothering and my dad will talk your ear off about the history of the bay, but no matter what, they're going to love you."

She turned and looked at him, still not reassured.

"How do you know?"

He opened his mouth to speak but stopped himself. After clearing his throat, he smiled and began again. "Trust me." He lifted her hand and kissed her fingers, offering a quick wink, which brought the sunshine back to her beautiful brown eyes and the blush to her cheeks.

Mary McCandless left the stairs and walked quickly down the driveway.

Matt stepped out of the car and caught his mom in a hug to prevent her from overwhelming Elizabeth. With a quick look at his dad for help, he passed her off to Tom McCandless and ran around to open the car door, helping Elizabeth out. He stayed by her side as he made introductions.

"Mom, dad, this is Elizabeth Eaton."

"Welcome!" Mary McCandless engulfed Elizabeth in a warm hug. "We've got your room all ready. Oh, you poor thing!" she continued, leading Elizabeth past her husband who rolled his eyes and cast an amused look at his son.

"She's in good hands, Matt. No need to worry," he said, reaching out to pat his son's shoulder.

"I just don't want her to be scared off. Mom can be a bit much sometimes."

"It'll be fine. How was the trip down?"

Father and son trailed behind a mama hen with a newfound chick, climbing the steps and entering the house. Mary showed Elizabeth her room while Matt dropped his bag in his own. He waited until he heard his mom descend the stairs before knocking on the guestroom door.

Elizabeth glanced up from unpacking her bag. Matt stood just outside the doorway, his green eyes filled with both concern and excitement.

"You okay?"

She nodded and placed a stack of clothes in the top dresser drawer Mrs. McCandless had shown her.

"Yeah. A bit overwhelmed, I guess. Your mom is really nice."

Matt stepped inside. "She is. Need any help?"

She placed the last of her things in the drawer and set her backpack on the floor. "Nope. That was it."

"Cool. Well, come with me then. There's someone I want you to meet." He extended his hand.

Elizabeth's eyebrows shot up. His concern had given way to the excitement she'd glimpsed.

"What? Who? I don't think I'm ready..."

He grinned. "It'll be fine. I promise. Come on."

Matt led her down the stairs and out the back door. Elizabeth checked out the covered terrace as they passed through. It was decorated with four-season furniture; a whicker sofa and two matching chairs with blue cushions. Potted plants were placed with purpose around the area providing a pleasing visual aesthetic. Beyond the terrace, the backyard extended toward a sandy boundary. Past that was a rocky shoreline where the waves rolled in. The breeze from the Pacific ruffled her hair, the fresh scent of salty sea air tickling her nose. Matt turned left and headed for a shed at the edge of the property.

He stopped them just outside the double doors, and with a mischievous grin, asked her to close her eyes.

Not sure what to expect, Elizabeth shut them tight and waited.

She could hear him opening the doors followed by a scraping sound and a couple of grunts. Her brows came down and she bit her lip, worried now that some large, lumbering animal was about to pounce on her.

Matt blew out a breath and quickly dusted his hands off before returning to Elizabeth's side.

"Okay, are you ready?"

The excitement in his voice made her giggle. Whoever he was about to show her was obviously very important to him. That it was happening outside, at the shed, hinted it must be a beloved pet. But she didn't hear any barking. Surely, it was a dog...

"On the count of three, open your eyes," he said. "One, two, three!"

Elizabeth opened her eyes. She looked around. There was no dog. No cat even. No animal anywhere. Then she looked down. Confused, she cocked her head, then looked at Matt.

"You said "someone." All I see is a boat."

It was a small, white boat with an outboard motor. As far as she could tell, it had two seats. She didn't know much about boats. Well, she didn't know anything at all about boats, actually. What was she supposed to say?

Matt laughed at her confusion, but grabbed her hand and pulled her closer.

"Exactly," he said, then stopped next to it. "Elizabeth, this is Melissa. She's my very special girl."

Standing now at the side of the boat, Elizabeth could clearly see the name hand painted, in faded red letters. She'd heard of boys naming their cars after girls. Seems they named their boats too. But who was Melissa?

She smiled and cast him a sideways glance. "You wanted to introduce me to your boat?"

He looked at her expectantly. "Well, yeah." He shifted on his feet, seeing her confusion. "I've had her since I was sixteen. Some of my best memories are of summers out on the bay in my boat."

Understanding dawned. This was an important part of who he was, much like art was important to her.

"I see." She relaxed then. "Is this how you decided to go into marine biology?"

"It is, yeah. And I thought tomorrow I could take you out on the bay and show you. There's this pod of striped dolphins with a new baby. Maybe they'll show up."

"A baby? How cute!"

"Yeah, I named him George. He's a little character."

She clapped her hands, laughing out loud. "Sounds like fun. Now I can't wait to meet him and his family. I've read they're very intelligent."

Matt's enthusiasm grew. "Oh, they are. Just wait until you see how smart they are. I'll bring a bag of chum. They love that. We can feed them together."

"If they show up," she added.

He smiled. "I have a feeling they will." He looked out on the bay. "As long as the weather holds, we should be fine."

He turned back to her and gestured toward the house. "I guess we should head back inside. I have a feeling mom made a feast. Hope you're hungry."

She followed him, glancing back at the boat. "Don't you need to put it back in the shed?"

Matt shrugged. "Naw. She'll be fine," he said.

She?

Elizabeth shot him a wry look. "So, who is this Melissa, anyhow? First girlfriend?"

He chuckled. "Nope. Never dated anyone named Melissa. I just like the name. Always have."

"So, there's no real Melissa?" Elizabeth asked.

He turned back to her, blocking her way, a knowing smile on his lips. "No, no real Melissa. She's just my boat, but she means a lot to me."

"Oh," Elizabeth said, glancing down as he stepped closer.

He reached out to touch her cheek. "You mean a lot to me too. That's why I wanted to introduce you."

Her cheek tingled under his caressing fingertips. She looked up shyly, seeing the warmth radiating from his green eyes.

"I do?" Heat suffused her cheeks as he leaned in closer.

Matt's gaze took in the pink coloring her cheeks, then dropped to her lips. "You do." He closed the distance and kissed her, something he'd been wanting to do for hours.

His arms slid around her waist, and he pulled her against him. He held her tightly as he deepened the kiss, turning her knees to jelly.

Elizabeth melted into his arms and lost herself in the bliss of Matt's kisses. She felt hot even as the sea breeze cooled her skin and found herself desperately wanting to be closer still. Her arms wound around his neck and her fingers slid into the loose waves of his hair. It felt so familiar and yet so new.

"Dinner!"

A voice broke through the haze of passion bringing them back to reality that they were standing in the middle of the backyard, entwined.

Matt ended their kiss and rested his chin on top of her head. Several calming breaths later, he chuckled.

"Well timed, mom. Well timed."

Elizabeth laughed, then whispered, "Do you think she saw us?"

He rubbed her back. "Yeah, probably."

Embarrassment crept up her neck. "I don't think I can face her now."

He pulled away and took her hands. "Don't worry. I'll be right there by your side. Besides, I'm sure she's thrilled."

He turned and, still holding her hand, led the way back to the house.

"That's a strange thing to say. Why would she be thrilled?" Elizabeth asked, staying close to his side.

He looked at her upturned face and smiled before quickly kissing the tip of her nose.

"Because you're the first girl I've ever brought home."

Elizabeth spent the rest of the day floating on a cloud of happiness. She enjoyed dinner with Matt's parents, and they played board games after, laughing and getting to know each other. In between rolls of the dice, the blush returned to her cheeks, much to her chagrin, as Matt caught her eye across the dining room table. The slow smile that spread across his lips each time reminded her of the sizzling kisses they shared in the backyard earlier. And when he walked her to her bedroom door that night, she wondered how in the world she would ever get any sleep knowing it would be hours before they could be together again. It didn't matter that he was just across the hall. Knowing this only made the hours pass slower and increased her desire to be in his arms once again. As the downstairs clock struck midnight, the occupants in the bedrooms above did not notice as dreams unfurled, revealing another time, another place; both unknown, yet familiar. And as the last chime sounded, outside, a car rolled to a stop at the end of Marine Street. The engine went silent, and the headlights winked out.

Chapter 17

The new day dawned dreary beneath a cloudy sky. The light mist that fell in the pre-dawn hours cleared up by mid-morning leaving behind a coating of moisture upon the air that clung to the grass and dampened the earth, but it could not dampen Elizabeth's spirits. Matt was waiting for her when she walked into the kitchen, a quick breakfast of eggs and toast already prepared.

"We'll leave as soon as you're finished," he said, a joyful smile on his face.

Elizabeth sat at the table and picked up her fork. "You're not eating?" she asked.

He shook his head. "Already did. I'm just going to pack up some snacks and bottled water for us and then go fish out a bag of chum from the spare fridge in the garage. I had dad pull down a frozen bag last night. Should be fully thawed by the time we get out into the bay."

She chewed her eggs and glanced out the window.

"Looks a bit overcast," she observed.

Matt's eyes followed her line of sight, and he shrugged. "Pretty much par for the course around here. The weather app shows scattered storms later, but we'll be back by then. No worries, Miss Eaton, this isn't my first time in a boat," he said, leaning down to drop a quick kiss on her lips. "Finish up and meet me out back."

He left her holding her fork, another hot blush stealing up her neck and suffusing her cheeks.

She ate quickly, downing a glass of milk and then washed her dishes, setting them in the drain board. She didn't want to leave a mess for Mrs. McCandless. After she dried her hands on the dish towel, she headed out the back door. The air was thick with humidity, but the sea breeze blowing in off the bay made it tolerable. Elizabeth glanced down at her jean shorts, pink t-shirt, and pink sneakers hoping her attire was sufficient for the trip. She pulled out a pair of sunglasses from her pocket and slid them on her face, then reached up and tightened her ponytail. In the distance, she saw Matt pulling the boat across the sandy, rocky beach. He waded out, dragging it further into the surf. She smiled as she noted the muscles in his arms flexing with the effort.

He wore a dark blue t-shirt paired with khaki cargo shorts. He was barefoot as he dragged the boat named Melissa over the sand and into the water. As the boat now bobbed up and down in the waves, she realized she was going to have to remove her own shoes to get in or else ruin her favorite pink sneakers. He turned and waved, gesturing for her to join him.

With a deep sigh, she waved back and walked across the yard to the beach beyond. There, she sat and began removing her shoes and socks while Matt chuckled.

"Well, I can't ruin my favorites," she said, one shoe off.

"Can't have that," he agreed. Then he came out of the water and before she could protest, he scooped her up in his arms and carried her to the boat.

"Matt, put me down!" she laughed.

"Just hold onto that shoe, gorgeous." He waded in and set her on the first bench in the boat. That act was followed by a sweet kiss and sexy smile from him that made her knees weak. Good thing she was already sitting down!

She had to admit, being with him was exciting. Wasn't it every girl's dream to have a strong, handsome boyfriend capable of carrying her like she weighed nothing at all? She slipped her shoe back on as he turned the boat around and then pulled himself in, tilting the craft sideways and causing her to grab the seat so she didn't fall out. A pair of flip flops awaited him on the floor of the boat. He left them there and reached instead for the oars lying along the inside.

"Gotta row out a bit before I can crank the motor. Once we get past the seaweed, it'll be smooth sailing," he said.

She nodded and held on, watching him from behind her shades. The bay leading out to the Pacific was beautiful, but she only had eyes for the handsome young man sitting across from her, pulling the oars and propelling them through the surf. His broad shoulders and defined biceps held her attention almost as much as the twinkle in his eyes.

The slow smile that spread across his lips told her he knew she was watching him. Heat scorched her cheeks as she glanced away and saw the shoreline growing distant.

As soon as they got past the seaweed and into deeper water, Matt stowed the oars, switched seats with her, and then reached behind him to pull the cord. The motor sputtered to life, and they were off! Wind whipped her ponytail and cooled her face as the boat sped through the deep blue water of the bay.

Matt steered them west, then turned south. She couldn't even see the house anymore, which made her nervous, but she trusted that Matt knew where they were going and would bring them back safely. She tried to relax and just enjoy the adventure. Out here on the waves, all the trouble and drama from the incident at school faded away. Her ruined painting didn't matter. Angelica and her weird obsession didn't matter. All that mattered was this moment, and the sweet young man who'd entered her life and changed it for the better. A month ago, she'd been single and focused on work and classes. Now she had a boyfriend, and everything felt different. This week spent with him, away from both school and work, was a turning point. It was incredibly exciting, and yet oddly familiar.

Nearly an hour later, Matt cut the engine. They'd arrived, apparently. If she squinted, she could see a shoreline in the distance, but where they dipped and bobbed in the boat, the water was deep blue and choppy.

"This is the spot," he announced, lowering the anchor.

Elizabeth wasn't certain the rope was long enough after looking over the side. The water appeared deep, and she couldn't see the bottom.

"Don't worry," he chuckled, reading her thoughts. "There are rocks below and the anchor usually catches. It'll keep us stable enough while we're out here."

She shook her head. "So, this is where George and his family are?" She glanced around.

"Hopefully. There's no guarantee. They might've moved on, but we'll see." Matt reached under the seat and pulled out two coolers. He opened the first one and handed her a bottle of water. "Hydration is important," he reminded her.

After setting his own aside, he opened the second cooler and lifted out a large plastic bag. He unzipped it and began dumping the contents over the side. The smell of fish hit her nose, and she made a face.

Matt laughed. "I know, it stinks, but the dolphins love it. If they're nearby, this will bring them here. They have a great sense of smell."

"Ugh." Elizabeth covered her nose until Matt finished emptying the chum. He rinsed the baggie in the seawater and then put it back inside the second cooler and shut the lid. The smell of fish eventually faded, and she popped the cap on her bottled water, taking a swig.

They sat quietly, floating on the ocean, watching the water for any sign of curious striped mammals.

Before long, they were enjoying the peanut butter and jelly sandwiches Matt made for them and sharing stories of their childhoods. When more than an hour passed, a rumble in the distance alerted them to the coming storm.

Elizabeth looked behind her toward the horizon. Dark clouds were rolling in from the sea. A flash of lightning arced toward the water followed by another crack of thunder. She looked at Matt.

"We should get back," she said, a nervous edge in her voice. Being caught out on the water in a storm sparked a shiver of fear.

Matt nodded. "Yeah. I guess our dolphin friends aren't coming. Probably knew about the weather before we did." He glanced at his watch. "The weather app said it wouldn't hit until later. Guess it's moving faster than they thought." He shrugged and turned, reaching for the rope, preparing to hoist the anchor.

Elizabeth busied herself closing the cooler of snacks and pushed it under the seat. When she looked up again, Matt was struggling with the rope.

"What's wrong?" she asked.

He sighed and tugged again. "I think it's stuck. Hold on," he said, twisting around to pull it in the opposite direction. He gave it a good yank and it gave. But the look on his face changed quickly from relieved to surprised.

"Crud," he muttered as he continued to pull up the rope. He was reeling it in fast now, his eyes wide.

"What is it?" Elizabeth asked, her anxiety spiking.

Matt pulled in the last of the rope…with no anchor tied to the end. He stared at the frayed cordage.

"I don't understand," he said. "This was a new rope. Looks like something cut right through it."

"The rocks?" she asked.

He shook his head. "No. They aren't sharp here. Mostly rounded and smooth. This has never happened before."

"Do you think some sea creature chewed through it?" Elizabeth had no knowledge of what type of sea creature might be able to chew through thick rope, but something had either eaten it or, according to Matt's words, cut through it.

"No way. Fish usually leave the rope alone and larger mammals don't bother with it either." He touched the frayed threads of rope, his expression flummoxed. Finally, he shook his head. "Well, looks like I need a new anchor." He glanced out to sea. "And we need to be getting back. Those dark clouds are getting closer fast."

She followed his line of sight and felt another shiver shoot down her spine. "Will we make it back in time?" she asked, worried they'd be caught in the downpour.

He pointed north where the sky was still blue. "We'll be ahead of the storm the whole way. Should get back to the house before the first drops fall on us."

Elizabeth swallowed her relief. "Good. Okay. Let's go then."

He smiled and reached out to pat her hand. "Don't worry. I've got you."

Matt twisted around and reached for the cord. It took a few tries, but the motor sputtered to life. He rotated the tiller and steered them back toward Tillamook.

The wind picked up, whipping their hair more on the return trip and creating rough waves. Matt turned west to avoid the reef, taking them out into deeper water. Once clear, he steered them around intending to ride back nearer the distant shoreline where it would be safer. As the boat turned back east, the motor hiccupped, sputtered, and died.

Surprised, Matt turned and began pulling the starter cord...again, and again, and again, to no avail.

"What's wrong? Why did the motor stop?" Elizabeth asked.

"Don't know," he said, pulling the cord again.

"Are we out of gas?"

He shook his head. "I filled it up before we left. We should have plenty of gas." He looked at the gauge.

It was empty.

"What the hell?" The words spilled from his lips before he could stop himself.

"What? What is it?" Elizabeth leaned forward.

Matt was shaking his head now in disbelief. He swallowed hard and looked at her.

"Uh, it's empty. The gas tank is empty." His expression was one of complete shock.

"How? You just said you filled it before we left!" Elizabeth's stomach rolled reminding her of that moment on a rollercoaster when the car pauses at the top and then plummets down, down, down.

"I did. I promise you, I did!" Matt looked again at the gas gauge and then pulled the cord repeatedly, praying it was just a malfunction of the instrument. The motor refused to start. He looked behind them at the approaching storm, and then toward the distant shore. It was at least two miles away. There was nothing for it except to row them in. But in these increasingly choppy waves, and with the current, it was going to be a challenge. He caught Elizabeth's eye and saw the raw fear in them. He had to protect her. There was no other choice.

He picked up the oars and slid them through the oarlocks, tightening them. "I'm going to row us to the shore. We'll have to hunker down there until the storm passes. Maybe I can get dad to drive down and pick us up."

She nodded and looked over her shoulder. "Will we make it?"

He looked back at the dark sky. A loud boom caused them both to jump.

"I hope so," he said, and then looked at her again. "We need to switch seats." He moved to the side and helped her cross over. "I think you should get down on the floor and hold on. The waves are getting higher. Put this on." He tossed her a life jacket as he reached under his seat for the spare. His hand came up empty.

"What about you?" she asked, settling onto the floor of the shell and tightening the belt of the jacket.

His eyes frantically searched the floor of the boat but found only two coolers and Elizabeth. He swallowed hard, mentally chastising himself for not double-checking the life jackets before they left.

"I'll be all right. Don't worry. Just hold on, okay?" Matt settled onto the seat, his back facing the shore. Without waiting a moment more, he put his back into it and dug the oars into the choppy water and pulled.

Her hands shook as she gripped the steering wheel. The drive back to Portland took longer than expected. The storm blowing in off the Pacific snarled traffic out of Tillamook as residents hurried home and others visiting from the big city tried to beat the weather. But it wasn't the line of traffic in front of her she saw, it was what she'd witnessed that morning.

She'd been hiding behind two tall pines on the edge of the McCandless property. It was from that vantage point she saw Matt drag the boat out to the water. And when he saw *her* come out of the backdoor, a ridiculous smile had spread across his handsome face, a face she'd been seeing in her dreams since she'd first laid eyes on him in Mr. Jeffries' classroom. Those dreams were vivid and intense, filled with happy and loving vignettes of the two of them together, seen always through her own eyes, meeting for the first time in high school, holding hands, making plans, making love... But although the dreams felt familiar, felt like memories, she knew none of it was real. They'd only just met. But the dreams pulled her in, made her so happy, until she awoke. Then, heartbreak consumed her. She didn't understand any of it. She only knew what her heart wanted, and it wanted Matt McCandless. So, she'd set out to make that happen.

But he rejected her.

Worse, he'd rejected her for someone unworthy. It was unfathomable. How could he possibly choose that simple, average girl over a woman like herself? Elizabeth Eaton wouldn't know what to do with such a magnificent young man like Matt! But she knew!

Still, her efforts to snare his attention failed, and the rage that filled her had boiled over like a pot of water left on the stovetop unchecked. It surprised her still what she'd done, but not so much as what she'd done last night. Angelica gritted her teeth and pressed down harder on the gas pedal. The line of traffic in front of her opened up and she merged onto the highway, maneuvering around another car as the dark clouds above let loose their payload.

She'd almost decided to reveal herself, to run to Matt and urge him not to go out in the boat. Seeing him standing in the shallows, the wind whipping through his wavy blond hair and plastering his t-shirt against the muscles on his chest and arms, had filled her with equal parts desire and regret. Anger wasn't the answer. Harming him wasn't the answer. She just needed to try harder, make him see her. Surely, this attraction wasn't one-sided. It couldn't be! It felt too real, like destiny. She'd convinced herself to step out of the shadows, make herself known. She'd figure out some story, some excuse as to why she was there. He would see through it, of course, but he would understand, and he would fall in love with her as soon as he realized they were meant to be together. Her heart swelled with hope.

And then *she* walked out the backdoor and it all came rushing back.

Matt had brought Elizabeth to his home. Not her. He'd spent the entire night inside his parents' house with Elizabeth. Not her. He was now taking the boat out for a romantic ride with Elizabeth. Not her.

She'd retreated again to the shadow of the pines, watching as the man she wanted more than life itself picked that simpering girl up in his strong arms and carried her out to the waiting boat. She watched, rage bubbling up once again, as they laughed with such joy. She bit her lip until it bled when he kissed her to suppress the primal scream threatening to escape. And when he rowed them out to deeper water and cranked the motor, the light in her eyes dimmed and a wicked smile spread across her face. They deserved what was coming. If she couldn't have him, the simpering girl would not have him either.

And with that, she had slipped from her hiding spot and run down the street to her car. She'd driven away from Marine Street as fast as possible, not once looking back. It was done. Over. There was nothing left except to finish it.

She replayed the dreams in her mind of her and Matt together, smiling sadly. They could have been so happy. Should have been. But he didn't want her, he wanted Elizabeth. He wanted the broken girl, the crippled one. *The crippled one?* The visions from her dreams became convincingly real and her mind let go, becoming unmoored from the present. She knew what she had to do now.

Resolute, peace filled her.

"I love you... *Wade*," she murmured.

Angelica pressed the gas pedal to the floor and let go of the steering wheel as tears filled her eyes, blurring the headlights of the oncoming car.

Chapter 18

The harder he rowed, the further from shore they seemed to drift. His shoulders aching and his muscles cramping, Matt doubled his efforts, fighting the current pulling them out to sea.

The storm was in full effect now and he struggled to quell the panic rising inside. His eyes sought Elizabeth's. She was huddled on the floor, gripping the seat. Her ponytail was dripping wet, and tendrils of dark brown hair were plastered to her terrified face. Her fear ate at him as he fought to avoid the waves now washing into the boat. *The Melissa* wouldn't last much longer if he couldn't get them to shore. If the riptide succeeded in pulling them out to sea, they were done. He couldn't let that happen, couldn't fail her.

"It's going to be okay, Elizabeth," he said, his words far more confident than he felt.

Her teeth chattered as the now much colder sea water splashed over the stern. Between it and the rain, there was no escaping getting soaked.

"Are we almost there?" she asked, her voice shaking as lightning zipped overhead followed by a loud crack of thunder.

Matt cringed and then glanced over his shoulder. The rain was falling in sheets now and he could no longer see the shoreline.

"Almost," he said, hoping it was true, although deep down inside, he knew otherwise.

He faced her once again, noticing that the water inside the boat was nearly six inches deep. They were in trouble. Big trouble. And he didn't know what to do. They had no gas, no anchor, and no possible way to reach land with the current driving them out to sea. Without further thought, he pulled the oars inside and secured them in their locks. Then, he abandoned his seat and joined Elizabeth on the floor, wrapping his arms around her and holding her tight.

"We'll just have to ride it out and hope the waves push us the rest of the way in," he said, putting as much conviction into the statement as possible. If he could will it, it would happen, and they would arrive, safe and sound, on the rocky beach.

Elizabeth clung to him, tears welling in her eyes. "I'm scared."

Gently, he smoothed the wet strands of her hair back and cradled her cheek in his hand.

"Me, too. But we'll be okay. You'll be okay." His heart broke with each word. With every passing second, he knew it was a lie. "Elizabeth, I..."

The bow of the boat rose swiftly on a swell, going nearly vertical. The momentum rolled them both backwards, slamming them into the backseat.

"Matt!" Elizabeth screamed.

His arms tightened around her. "Hang on!"

The wave went higher, and then, just as suddenly as they went up, the wave receded and *The Melissa* came crashing down, flipping over.

Matt and Elizabeth were thrown into the mercurial water of the Pacific Ocean. Plunged beneath the surface, Elizabeth struggled to hold onto him. Matt's hands gripped her arms even as the forceful current pulled them apart. She opened her mouth to scream and swallowed the sea. Panicked, she twisted and felt his hands slip away.

Elizabeth broke the surface once again, gasping for breath and fighting to stay above water.

"Matt!" she screamed, twisting this way and that. "Matt!"

She could see the boat a good distance away before another wave crashed, taking it under. But still no sign of Matt.

"Please! Help me! Help! Matt! Matt!" Elizabeth screamed his name over and over again. Her legs cramped and her arms felt as if they weighed a hundred pounds each.

She was losing the battle. She called out for him again. "Matt! Answer me, please! Matt! I...I love you! Matt!" Her voice broke and her spirit followed.

A wave pushed her under, and she fought to rise. She barely got her mouth above water and sucked in the cool air before another wave slammed her back into the storm-tossed sea. The lights flickered inside her mind, flitting from one moment to the next in a montage of her life. Her mom and dad clapping when she revealed her first painting, her first day of school, her best friend Lacy laughing, and finally, Matt looking at her in that way that made her heart skip a beat. Those scenes bled one into the next, and then it all faded to black.

He heard her calling out to him but could not answer. He couldn't even open his eyes. Again, he heard her voice and terror zinged through his body, giving him just enough energy to lift his lids.

Light. So much light. It blinded him and he shut his eyes tight, trying to block it out.

Then he noticed the silence. The peace. The storm had passed. They made it to shore. They were safe!

He opened his eyes again and blinked rapidly, adjusting to the light. It was incredibly bright. He shielded his eyes and sat up carefully, looking around.

He was surrounded by white mist so thick; it reminded him of the fog that rolled into the bay at his parent's home. Matt stood and then ran his hands over his limbs checking for injuries. He found none, but did notice his clothes were dry. He must've been laying on the beach for quite a while. He must have...

Elizabeth!

Panic seized him and he spun around, searching for her.

"Elizabeth! Elizabeth, where are you?" He cupped his hands around his mouth and called out.

Fear gripping him, Matt began to run. He didn't know where he was going, couldn't even see the sand beneath his feet, but he ran anyway. He had to find her!

His eyes couldn't penetrate the thick mist. He stumbled, turning to try a different direction.

"Elizabeth!" he cried.

A dark form began to take shape ahead. Relieved, he pushed himself harder.

"Elizabeth! Is that you? Elizabeth!"

The figure turned toward him. It walked slowly, limping. She was hurt!

"Elizabeth!" he screamed, running toward her.

As he got closer, the mist lessened, revealing long, dark hair flowing as if on a gentle breeze. She wore pink, her favorite color, and now his. The nearer she drew, the more details he saw, like her big, brown eyes, and her sweet smile...

He froze. This wasn't Elizabeth. The face wasn't quite right. And she was shorter. But deep inside, he knew her. His heart knew her, and his soul rejoiced. Matt knew this face, had seen it in his dreams so many times, but those dreams had always faded away quickly, leaving only an impression.

She stopped before him, as surprised as himself.

Reaching out with a shaky hand, she touched his cheek. Tears filled her lovely eyes, and her lips trembled.

"Is it really you?"

The cosmic key turned, unlocking the truth. Memories flooded his mind in an avalanche of emotions.

His heart lurched in his chest, and he struggled to breathe. It couldn't be!

Trembling, he captured her hand and placed it over his runaway heart.

"Melissa?" he whispered.

Her eyes searched his, reflecting her disbelief, but nothing could hide the joy spilling down her cheeks in a river of tears.

"Wade!"

He pulled her into his arms and buried his face in her hair. Her scent, so familiar, filled him with longing. The memories continued to unfold. One, in particular, pained him to his soul. His arms tightened as sobs wracked his body.

"I'm so sorry, baby," he whispered, his breath hot against her ear. "I messed up. I should have been there," he cried. "I should have been there!"

"Sssh," she soothed. "You didn't know. You couldn't know. It was an accident. I shouldn't have gone out that night. But I tried, Wade. I tried so hard to get out, to get back to you, to tell you…"

She paused, the lump in her throat choking off her words.

He leaned back and searched her eyes. "To tell me what?"

Melissa swallowed hard. "To tell you…"

He saw it in her eyes, shining brighter than the white mist surrounding them. He touched her lips, shushing her as his heart overflowed.

"I know. I love you, too," he said. "I love you, Melissa. I knew it from the first moment I laid eyes on you. God, I've waited so long to say it. Never thought I'd get the chance. I prayed every day I'd somehow see you again, get to tell you just how much I've always loved you."

"Oh, Wade!" she cried.

He kissed her then, his lips crushing hers. All the love in his broken heart was poured into that kiss. She was his. And he was hers. Always. By some miracle, they'd found each other again, somewhere inside this bright white mist, where time held no meaning, and memories of their past life together were revealed and made perfect sense. She was his girl, and he'd waited a lifetime to tell her.

Something poked him in the back. Something cold…and wet. Fear snaked up his spine as he jerked his head around searching for…he didn't know what. The bright light flickered, and the mist shifted and rolled into loud, crashing waves. The soft pink material of Melissa's shirt was replaced by a thick life vest. Shocked, he pulled away and stared down into the face of Elizabeth Eaton.

"Wade? What's wrong?" she asked.

He blinked, confused, and suddenly panicked.

"Elizabeth?"

"Matt?" The joy in her eyes dimmed with each passing second. In its place, terror bloomed.

As the last of the white mist disintegrated, he realized they were running out of time in this in between world. Fast. He glanced down at his own body. No life vest. He remembered then. There was only one in the boat. He'd forgotten to check before they left. It was his fault. He looked at her again, seeing her ponytail flowing out behind her, seeing the face he knew now, in this life, once again.

The reality of their situation brought clarity…and resolve.

"You have to go back!" he said.

"What? No! Matt, no! I won't leave you!" she cried.

"Elizabeth, I love you, but you have to go back! I couldn't save you then, but I can save you now."

"No! Matt, no! I need you. Please, we only just found each other again! I love you!" Panic seized her.

He kissed her then, if only to calm her fears, and because letting her go would kill him. He blinked back tears and concentrated on the feel of her in his arms, the softness of her lips, and he thanked God for giving him this one last moment. And then, he pushed her away with all the strength in his body and soul, he pushed her up and away to the surface.

"No! Matt, no, please! I love you! I want to stay with you!"

He watched through a blur of unshed tears as she floated up. The mist dissolved and the waves took her, pulling her away until he could no longer see her sweet face.

"I love you, too," he whispered. "I will always love you. Live, baby. Please, live..."

Chapter 19

Gulls cried in the distance as frothy waves rolled gently upon the sandy beach, nudging her awake. Elizabeth opened her eyes, and then promptly rolled sideways, spitting up seawater. She coughed until her lungs were clear, and then looked around. She was on a rocky beach, still halfway in the water. She scooted back and carefully stood. Her knees wobbled and she noticed her feet were bare. Why were her feet bare?

She searched her memory, trying to make sense of it all. She'd been on a boat. A storm rolled in. She remembered being terrified, and then the boat capsized. She'd gone into the ocean and been tossed around like a rag doll before being pushed under by the powerful waves, the force of which had apparently pulled her shoes and socks right off. And she was still wearing a life jacket. The last thing she recalled was the feel of hands gripping her waist...

Matt! Oh, my God, Matt!

Matt didn't have a life jacket!

She turned, looking up and down the beach. There was no sign of him. No sign of anyone. Behind her was a stretch of forested land, and both to the north of the beach and south, no evidence of people, or lifeguard towers, or anything. She had no idea where she was or which way to go. She only knew she needed to find help, to find Matt.

At least the rain had stopped. It was the only thing in her favor now.

She felt tears stinging the backs of her eyes. *What do I do? Which way should I go?*

A chirping sound joined the cry of the gulls and the whoosh of the waves. As she stood drowning in indecision, the chirping grew louder. Tears spilled as she glanced around, trying to find the source. It was a familiar sound, but she couldn't place it. Where had she heard it before? What was it?

Elizabeth wiped the tears from her cheeks and turned south. The wind seemed to be blowing in that direction. Perhaps Matt had made it to shore, too, and was further down the beach. He might still be unconscious. He might need help. Fear and urgency welled within. She walked faster and called out.

"Matt!"

Chirp, chirp.

"Matt! Where are you? I'm here! Please, call out!"

She stumbled on a rock and fell to her knees. Pain shot up her leg and out of her mouth in a loud curse. She pressed her hands over the injury, noting a long scrape and bright red blood trickling down her shin.

It stung like hell and began to throb, but she couldn't let a scraped knee stop her.

Chirp, chirp, chirp.

She looked up, becoming increasingly annoyed with that sound. There was no one around, and even the crying gulls had flown away. Carefully, she arose and moved toward the water's edge. The saltwater would burn, but at least she'd clean some of the dirt and blood away. Elizabeth walked into the surf, getting in no deeper than just above her ankles. Her near drowning in the ocean made her leery of getting in any further. She leaned down and scooped up a handful of water, splashing it over the scrape. She winced and sucked in a breath. It hurt as much as she anticipated. Maybe even more. But the deed was done.

As she stood motionless waiting for the pain to pass, she stared out at the now calm Pacific. Where it had roiled angrily only a while ago—how long, she wasn't sure—intent on killing her, it seemed in this moment completely innocent of the attempt on her life. Still, she didn't trust it, not anymore. And she still did not know if the powerful ocean had claimed...

A sharp pain pierced her heart. No! She wouldn't accept that. Surely, he'd survived. He was strong, so strong! He'd done everything he could to save her, even giving her the only life jacket on the boat, a boat that had lost its anchor. A boat that had run out of gas.

Her lips twisted and her brow furrowed. How had any of that happened? Matt said he'd filled up the tank right before they left. How could a full tank just suddenly empty? And the rope that was once tied to the anchor had been cut.

Elizabeth's mind mulled over all these details. They'd only just arrived at the McCandless' home yesterday after discovering the violent destruction of her painting, after being warned by the dean to stay away until things calmed down, until the police could locate and question Angelica.

Angelica.

Elizabeth remembered then what the janitor said he'd overheard.

"She sounded pissed about the boy. Kept screaming "you won't take him from me again."

She had no idea what that meant then. But something tickled the back of her mind, something important. A certainty that it was all related began to manifest. There was a connection between her, Matt, and Angelica. Had they been followed to Tillamook? Had she sabotaged the boat?

If her line of thinking was correct, then it was possible Angelica had tried to kill them. She hadn't succeeded with Elizabeth, but Matt…

The tears returned but she wiped them away. There was no more time to waste. She had to get moving. She had to find Matt.

Chirp, chirp, chirp.

She looked up. In the shallows, a dolphin jumped and then swam in a circle before sticking its head out again.

They'd gone out that morning to see dolphins, to "meet" George, as Matt had explained. She swallowed hard past a lump in her throat. The dolphins never showed their faces. Now, one was making itself known, so it seemed.

"You're too late," she said, her voice raw.

Turning away, she headed south again, searching the beach for any sign of Matt. She navigated around giant rock formations to avoid the sharp stones beneath her feet. Progress was slow despite the urgency to find Matt or find help of any kind. The gray clouds overhead were thinning now and sunlight began to peek through. The increased visibility was welcome, but still, she found nothing. She walked on, wrapping her arms around her waist in a vain attempt to control her rising fear.

Nearly an hour down the beach and still no sign of Matt, no sign of life. As she looked ahead, there were only more of the large boulders sticking out of the water. Some were right along the edge of the shore; others were further out creating a dangerous barrier to anyone who might be boating or swimming. Whether a few feet to a few hundred feet between those furthest out and the shoreline, it didn't matter. She couldn't cover it all, and she wasn't even sure she'd chosen the right direction. As far as she knew, she'd just wasted a crucial hour going the wrong way.

Hopelessness swamped her and Elizabeth cried out. "Matt! Maaaatt!

The raw scream came from within her very soul. Sobs wracked her body, and she gave in to her deepest fear. She'd lost him, after only just finding him.

She crumpled to the ground, her grief tearing her apart.

Pounding the rough sand with her fists, she screamed, over and over again, until she couldn't scream anymore.

"Hey! Lady, are you okay?"

Elizabeth jerked, pulled from her pain. She looked up and saw two young men with long, black hair coming down the beach. They looked Tillamook.

As they drew closer, she could see they were young, maybe fifteen or sixteen.

"What happened to you?" the shorter one asked.

Elizabeth trembled, her relief at being found overridden by her grief.

"Please, help me! We were caught in the storm. Our boat went down."

The taller boy looked around. "We?"

She nodded. "My boyfriend, Matt…"

The shorter boy dropped down beside her and patted her back. "It's okay. We'll help you. Where's your boyfriend?"

The tears welled like pools in her eyes. "I can't find him. Please help me. I need to find Matt."

"Okay, okay," the boy soothed. He looked up at his friend. "What do we do?"

"Call the tribal police for help," the taller boy said.

Chirp. Chirp, chirp, chirp.

The taller boy, with an angular, serious face, grew quiet and watched as a dolphin poked its head out of the surf and chirped at them. It was only a few feet out in the shallows.

"What is it?" the shorter boy asked.

The tall one didn't answer at first. He watched as the dolphin chirped again, then dove under the water and swam a short distance away, breaching the surface every few feet. It swam to one of the boulder outcroppings, jumped high into the air, and then swam back again where it repeated its antics.

"It followed me," Elizabeth said.

"What?" The taller boy asked.

"I saw it back where I washed up on the beach. At least, I think it's the same one. It did that, kept making that sound."

The shorter boy stood. "Why is it doing that?"

The taller boy stepped closer to the shoreline, his eyes tracking the dolphin as it made the circuit again.

"It's trying to tell us something." He turned to Elizabeth. "Where did you first see it again?"

She pointed north. "We left out of the bay behind Matt's house in Tillamook. I don't know where I landed, or even where I am."

"You're in Neskowin, just about forty-five minutes south." The taller boy walked closer to the edge. "It's definitely trying to tell us something. Weird. I'm going to go check."

Elizabeth's heart lurched as the boy began to take off his shoes. "What? No! It's dangerous!"

He offered a reassuring smile. "It's not that deep out there. I'll be okay." He looked at his friend, serious once again. "Call the police, Avery. Get someone out here for her."

The shorter boy already had his cellphone in hand. He dialed and waited as it rang. Elizabeth watched as the taller boy entered the water and waded out. The dolphin chirped loudly, seemingly excited that the boy was following. It swam again toward the rocky outcropping, this time waiting patiently. By the time the taller boy arrived, Elizabeth could see that the water was only up to his chest. He moved carefully to the cluster of boulders. The dolphin chirped louder, swimming now around to the far side facing out into the ocean. The boy followed and then climbed up onto a lower rock. He stood and maneuvered carefully over and around the sharp, slippery granite clusters.

Minutes passed. She couldn't see him and panic set in.

Then, he peeked around the edge of the largest boulder and shouted.

"There's a body! Avery, get help! Hurry!

A body...

His words sunk in, and Elizabeth's world shattered into a million heartbroken pieces.

Chapter 20

Three Months Later...

It was quiet in the classroom. No one was around on Saturdays save for the janitorial staff and a few professors catching up on their end of semester grading. But the art room was empty except for one. Elizabeth concentrated as she blended wisps of Titanium white over an underpainting mixture of Payne's and Davy's gray. It was the final section, and with one last stroke, she stood back, wiping the brush on a cloth.

She stared at the completed work. Silently, she took in the composition, painted entirely from memory.

He stood, his strong, bare body in profile, as if about to walk away, and his face turned toward the viewer. Emerald-green eyes filled with raw emotions were set in a handsome face framed by dark blond, wavy hair. He was surrounded by a swirling white mist within a cell of thunderous, dark clouds. It was how he appeared in her dreams now.

It was the way she began to draw him, and then created this painting, a painting she owed Mr. Jeffries for her class assignment.

She'd spent nearly all her Saturdays since that day at the university working on it.

Now, it was finished, and she was filled with both relief that it was done, and sadness each time she viewed him standing there, lost in the mist of time. It was something she still didn't understand, the dreams that came after. What those dreams revealed felt like someone else's life, but at the same time, she knew it was her own, a previous life, one unfinished.

So much had changed since then.

The boat had been recovered ashore about five miles from where she'd been located. A preliminary investigation showed the gas tank on the motor had been punctured. That news was followed by the report that Angelica Mason, age twenty-four, had died in a head-on collision two miles outside of Tillamook. Police concluded, with the confirmation of traffic cameras, that she'd been in the area at the time and that there was probable cause, aided by the incident report from the university, that she'd attempted to sabotage the boat, which led to them running out of gas, and no doubt, the cutting of the anchor as well. All of which caused the unfortunate tragedy. As far as the police were concerned, the case was now closed.

But Elizabeth would never forget, nor forgive.

She'd suffered unspeakable trauma. She still had trouble sleeping, and often, she awoke crying out into the darkness.

Tears stung her eyes, and one slipped down her cheek. She sniffed and shook herself.

"What's wrong, babe?"

Arms slid around her waist and the sadness threatening to engulf her retreated. She sighed and leaned back into Matt's embrace.

His warmth surrounded her, and her heart skipped a beat. She cherished every single cuddle now.

A small smile touched her lips. "Nothing. Just reflecting."

He kissed her cheek and rested his chin on her shoulder.

"It's finished?"

She nodded. "Yep. All done."

He held her quietly as he took it in.

"So, that's how you see me, huh? Kinda god-like, I think. Am I really that goodlooking?"

She chuckled and reached back to swat his hip.

He laughed and tightened his hold.

"Now, now. Hands off the goods, ma'am. I'm a model now."

"You wish!" Elizabeth set the paintbrush and cloth down and turned in his arms to face him.

Matt sighed and then grew serious. "You still having those dreams?"

She nodded and laid her cheek against his chest. "Yeah. Can't really make sense of them. But they're not scary anymore. At least, not as much. I mean, when I wake up, you're there, so I know they can't be true. I haven't lost you."

Matt stroked her hair and kissed the top of her head. "You'll never lose me. You're my girl, Elizabeth, and I love you."

She smiled. "Yes, I am. I love you, too."

His eyes wandered over the painting. He, too, had dreams now of her surrounded in a white mist. But he hadn't shared that fact. When she first told him of the recurring dreams, he'd been in shock. How could two people have nearly the same dreams about something that could not possibly have happened? He had no answer and did not want to freak her out any further. But he had been freaked out himself. He'd spent a few weeks in hospital after being found unconscious on the rocks in the bay of Neskowin. Nearly drowned, the doctors who treated him had no idea how long he'd been unconscious or how long he might have been deprived of oxygen. He still couldn't believe either of them had survived. More unbelievable was the story told by two local boys to television reporters and journalists about *how* they found him.

As the thought crossed his mind, his eyes discovered something hidden in the mist behind him in the portrait. Barely noticeable was a tiny dolphin, its little face peeking out.

He pointed. "Hey, is that George?"

She turned, and grinned. "I couldn't resist. He's the reason you're here with me now. I had to give him credit."

Matt chuckled. "Immortalized forever. My hero." He shook his head. When police and Search and Rescue arrived, one of them had taken pictures for their report. None of them believed the Tillamook boys until the dolphin reappeared while S&R lifted his body off the rocks and into a waiting RHIB, or rigid hull inflatable boat. The little gray guy chirped happily and swam circles around the rescue team as they pulled the boat back to shore. Then, he swam off.

When Matt awoke in the hospital, he'd seen the news on the TV in his room and he'd recognized George. Knowing he'd been saved by the friendly dolphin, and probably his family, stunned him. Somehow, they'd helped get him to shore, to safety, where he'd washed up on the lowest boulder in the cluster of large rocks in that bay. And George stayed near, desperately trying to find help. How he knew to find and follow Elizabeth was still a mystery, but he figured the dolphin pod had witnessed them capsizing and, as mind-blowing as the idea was, attempted to help them both. There was documented proof that dolphins communicate with each other using sophisticated language. He could only imagine that they organized to save both himself and Elizabeth and let each other know where the two humans washed up. When George discovered Elizabeth awake, he'd done everything in his power to get her attention and lead her to him.

Just...unbelievable.

Matt had yet to see his guardian angel. The idea of going back out on a boat held no appeal. Not yet anyhow. However, he knew it was just a matter of time. He had to get over the anxiety of the accident and near-death experience first. One day, he would get back out on the water. One day.

Right now, all he wanted was to be with Elizabeth. Before the accident, he knew he was falling in love with her. After the accident, he knew he'd loved her always, and for far longer than this lifetime. In the beginning, the memories scared the hell out of him. He spent too many nights in that hospital room, in the dark, listening to the monitor beep with every beat of his heart, trying to make it make sense that he loved Elizabeth, and Elizabeth was…Melissa. The first three days, he remembered everything, and it terrified him. On the fourth day, the memories began to fade. Now, he had only vague recollections, like a dream he would try to remember but the details remained out of reach. After a week, he'd convinced himself it had all been a dream. But three months later, he still awoke in the middle of the night, fresh from seeing her again, surrounded by a white mist, looking like his Elizabeth, but also, like someone else, someone his heart told him was also her.

He worried he might be going crazy, but then Elizabeth was there, by his side, and everything was right in his world once again.

Matt shook himself. He wasn't a religious person, but he always believed that there were things in this life, in this world, in the broader universe, that humans would never understand, could never understand. These cosmic secrets were too extraordinary for the brain to comprehend. So, he left those thoughts alone and focused on the here and now. The beautiful young woman in his arms was something he understood. She was someone important to him, that he loved and cherished. Nothing mattered more than this and he wouldn't waste time he could spend with her on searching for answers he'd never find.

He was happy and they were together. Whatever the reason, and however it came about, they'd found each other. Their love was the greatest gift.

"What are you thinking about?" she asked, looking up at his pensive face.

He turned his attention to her, struck by her beauty and the love shining in her warm, brown eyes. "You. Always you." He kissed her then, softly and sweetly. "Now that your painting is finished and the semester is over, what would you like to do, Miss Elizabeth Eaton?" he asked, smiling that slow smile that always made her knees weak.

A blush crept up her cheeks. "Celebrate, I guess? But something small, just you and me."

His hands caressed her back, causing the heat in her cheeks to spread like wildfire throughout her body. He loved seeing her reaction to him. He loved her pink cheeks. Pink, her favorite color, and now, forever his.

"Okay, babe. Just you and me," he replied, and then thought...

For a lifetime...and then some.

The End

Book Freebie!

The Angelic Hosts Series is an epic romantic supernatural fantasy saga in progress. Subscribe to my Substack (FREE) at

micheleegwynn.substack.com

and read books 1 through 4 of the Angelic Hosts series today! Fall in love with the angels. (Subscribe in episode one.)

Begin reading *Camael's Gift*, Episode One, right now! (At the top of the landing page)

In the heavenly realms a war is raging between good and evil as the prophesy unfolds. A new messiah will return. A little child shall lead them all...

> *"(Gwynn)She is a talented author that really knows how to weave the intricate tapestry of a book..." ~ JMB*

<u>Camael's Gift, The Introduction:</u> If he chooses her, he'll be damned for eternity.

From the moment the archangel Camael set eyes upon Hannah Adams, his heart was forever hers. For Cam, there was never any other choice. He would defy heaven itself, fall from His grace and accept becoming one of the Dark Ones, all for one sweet moment with the human woman. But he's not the only one who wants her. The Fallen have targeted Hannah as well. Plotting to obtain the key to free Lucifer from the pit of a thousand years, a Dark One makes himself known to the young, grieving mother. Her life now in peril, Camael finds himself ordered to protect her at all costs to save mankind and prevent the Fallen from unleashing Hell on Earth.

<u>Camael's Battle:</u> If the prophesy is fulfilled, the unborn savior will die...

In love, and about to become a father for the first time, the archangel Camael finds himself living a nightmare when his beloved Hannah goes missing. The goddess, Astarte, is orchestrating her fallen lover Lucifer's release from hellish incarceration and secrets long buried will be revealed causing chaos and throwing obstacles into Camael's path to rescuing his true love. Even with help from the rebellious Gabriel, and reluctant Michael, he might not make it in time. Can Camael save Hannah and their unborn child, or will Lucifer rise from the pit to lead an army of darkness into battle for dominion over the heavens and the Earth?

<u>Sophie's Wish:</u> An Act of Kindness Sets an Ancient Prophesy in Motion...

Five years have passed since the archangel Camael left a newborn baby on the doorstep of Charles and Nanette Fairchild. A child of destiny, Sophie amazes her parents and collects strays, all while lovingly watched over by her two invisible, winged guardians, Uncle Cam and Uncle Gabriel. Now, she has befriended another stray, a homeless girl--a victim of multiple tragedies, far too many for one so young. By bringing the girl home, Sophie's act of kindness heralds the unfolding of an ancient prophesy, one that ensures the downfall of the Dark Ones should it be allowed to play out. Desperate, the Fallen rise determined to prevent the prophesy from being fulfilled by killing the messenger...the child of destiny herself! Can Sophie's angelic uncles save her before it's too late?

<u>Nephilim Rising:</u> The archangel Gabriel has been busy over the millennia and Antonio Diaz, a Marine Sergeant—and something else not quite human—is the result. And now he's the new guardian!

Following news of his father's passing, unbelievable secrets are revealed tearing a Marine's world apart. With the full blood moon rising soon, Sgt. Antonio Diaz faces a battle the likes of which the combat soldier has never seen, nor is he prepared.

Blanca Ramos grew up the hard way, an orphan caring for her little brother as they bounced from one foster family to the next. Harassed by a local drug dealer, she fears for her safety. When Blanca's brother goes missing, she confronts the thug embroiling herself in a dangerous situation she cannot win. Saved by a handsome stranger Blanca finds herself attracted to her rescuer. But Antonio has a terrifying secret, one that will forever change her destiny.

An ancient prophesy unfolding sends earth-bound demons scrambling for dominion over Hell. With the help of an army of angels, Antonio must face the threat head-on to save both Blanca's life...and his soul!

Also By Michele E. Gwynn

Visit my website for these books plus updates on upcoming releases! micheleegwynnauthor.com.

Checkpoint Novels

Exposed: The Education of Sarah Brown (novel)

The Evolution of Elsa Kreiss (novel)

The Redemption of Joseph Heinz (novel)

The Making of Herman Faust (prequel novella)

Green Beret Series

Rescuing Emma (18+)

Loving Leisl

Freeing Fatima

Saving Christmas

Loving Freddie

Saving Major Morgan (A Green Beret Series prequel novella)

The Soldiers of PATCH-COM

Secondhand Soldier (18+)

Second Chance Soldier

Second Breath Soldier

Silent Night Soldier

C'est la Vie Soldier

The Harvest Trilogy

Harvest

Hybrids

Census

Section 5 (A Harvest Trilogy Spinoff)

Stand Alones

Darkest Communion (Paranormal Romance, 18+)

Waiting a Lifetime (Contemporary Romance, Mystical)

Hiring John (Romantic Comedy 18+)

www.ingramcontent.com/pod-product-compliance
Lightning Source LLC
LaVergne TN
LVHW041702060526
838201LV00043B/541